IT WAS A RACE UNLIKE ANY THAT SI CWAN HAD SEEN BEFORE. . . .

Its skin looked like thick, dark leather, and it was clutching Si Cwan in a massive three-fingered hand. He didn't know what this creature was capable of, and he didn't want to take the time to find out. He drove both heels into the creature's face, staggering it by a grand total of about an inch and a half. Then the creature spoke to him:

"I am *Excalibur* security chief Zak Kebron," the creature said, "and you are under arrest."

STAR TREK®
NEW FRONTIER

BOOK TWO

INTO THE VOID

PETER DAVID

POCKET BOOKS
New York   London   Toronto   Sydney   Tokyo   Singapore

An *Original* Publication of POCKET BOOKS

POCKET BOOKS, a division of Simon & Schuster Inc.
1230 Avenue of the Americas, New York, NY 10020

This book is published by Pocket Books, a division of
Simon & Schuster Inc., under exclusive license from
Paramount Pictures.

ISBN: 0-671-01396-3

First Pocket Books printing July 1997

10 9 8 7 6 5 4 3 2 1

POCKET and colophon are registered trademarks of
Simon & Schuster Inc.

Printed in the U.S.A.

THE
EXCALIBUR

Captain's Personal Log, Stardate 50923.1. "Captain." Captain Mackenzie Calhoun. I thought I had left the Fleet forever behind me, and yet now I find myself not only back in the Fleet, but commanding a starship.

The Excalibur *is currently a hive of activity. She's an Ambassador-class ship, registry number 26517. Funny. I've only been on her for a few hours, and I'm already taking pride in her. Not all crew members have yet reported in, but the final work is even now approaching its completion. I have spoken extensively with Chief Engineer Burgoyne 172, and s/he assures me that we will be ready to launch for Sector 221-G on the expected date. Burgoyne is the first Hermat I've ever met, and frankly, s/he's odd even for a*

Hermat. But s/he definitely knows engines, and that's what counts.

I still can't believe I'm here. When I was a young "rebel" on my native Xenex—battling the Danteri to try and drive those damned oppressors off my planet—I never dreamed of anything beyond the confines of my homeworld. It was Jean-Luc Picard who came to me when we were on the cusp of winning our long battle with the Danteri. He saw something in me, something that he felt should be shaped and honed into a Starfleet officer. I will never forget when he told me of the noted Earthman, the Great Alexander, who supposedly wept when he realized that he had no new worlds to conquer. There I was, having accomplished the liberation of my people before I was twenty years old. Picard realized that if I allowed that to be the pinnacle of my life, that it would not go well for me in later years. He is the one responsible for my seeking out my true destiny.

Damn the man.

I try to live my life without regrets. I did not regret resigning from Starfleet, for it was what I had to do at the time. And now I am determined not to regret rejoining. If nothing else, Picard was correct about the reaction of Admiral Jellico. Upon learning that I had been given command of the Excalibur, *with the mandate to explore the fallen Thallonian Empire of Sector 221-G and provide humanitarian effort whenever possible, Jellico looked angry enough to shred a Borg with his teeth. He's going to have to deal with it, however. That's his problem, not mine. My problem is to focus my attention on the job at hand, and not let my core impatience with the rigmarole and high-mindedness of Starfleet interfere with my job.*

Several major bits of business need to be attended to. I am still awaiting the arrival of Lieutenant Soleta, my science officer. She's had experience in Thallonian space. Even though Xenex is on the Thallonian/Danterian border, I possess only a smattering of knowledge about the territory. Soleta has actually been into the heart of that notoriously xenophobic realm and lived to tell of it. Her view of things will be invaluable. She is currently in San Francisco, teaching at the Starfleet Academy, but she should have received her orders by now and should be preparing to join us as soon as possible. Of the rest of my command staff, Dr. Selar is in the process of getting sickbay in fully operating condition. It's strange. I've worked with Vulcans before, and I'm well aware of their notorious reserve, but Selar is remote even for a Vulcan. So cold, so icy, so distant. I cannot help but wonder if she is simply overly dedicated to her Vulcan teachings, or if there is not something more going on in her head that I don't know about. Her medical performance is spotless and she came well recommended from Picard, who in turn heard nothing but good things about her from his own CMO. Picard's word is generally good enough for me, but to be blunt, Selar seems as if she'll have the bedside manner of a black hole, and I hope her presence here is not an error on my part.

Security Chief Zak Kebron is a Brikar, and certainly provides a feeling of security. I constantly have to request that he walk rather than run, since his running tends to make an entire deck vibrate. I've seen mountain ranges that are smaller. And yet he has astounding agility for someone who's got a hide tougher than twenty Hortas.

Astronavigator Mark McHenry comes highly recommended for helmsman, but he brings with him major caveats. I have very quickly learned that, during any conversation with Lieutenant McHenry, it seems as if he is either not listening at all, or listening to a conversation between two other people . . . neither of whom are in proximity. Yet he never seems to miss out on anything that's being said; how his mind is able to multitask in that way is a complete mystery to me.

Operations Officer Robin Lefler is recently promoted from Engineering. She seems very sociable . . . perhaps overly so, as if she's trying to compensate for something. "Desperately outgoing" would be the term I'd use. I'm having trouble getting a "read" on her, and will be keeping a weather eye on her for the time being.

The position of first officer remains open. I am finding the filling of that slot to be the most problematic area with which I have to deal. I have a number of worthy candidates, and have already interviewed several. Every single one has been eminently competent, knowledgeable, polite . . . and yet each of them seems a bit nervous around me. Intimidated, perhaps. They focus on my scar, the one I acquired in my youth when a Danterian laid open half my face. They seem to have trouble making eye contact. And they act as if at any moment I might start carving my initials in my desktop with the dagger I keep handy for senti-

mental reasons. I don't see why. It's my desk and my dagger, and if I happen to want to carve it into kindling, I damn well will.

Hmmm.

Clearly I will need a first officer whom I can not only tolerate, but who will also be able to tolerate me.

SHELBY

I.

ELIZABETH PAULA SHELBY gaped at Admiral Edward
Jellico. He could not have gotten a more stunned
reaction out of her if he'd suddenly ripped off his
own face and revealed himself to be a Gorn wearing
an exceptionally clever disguise.

Jellico was seated behind his desk, his fingers
steepled in front of him. He watched Shelby pace his
office with a mixture of amusement and awe. As
always, the woman seemed like a barely contained
dynamo of energy. When she was this upset, her face
tended to darken and provide such a contrast to her
strawberry blond hair that it looked as if her head
were on fire. Her ire, her astonishment, were so
inflamed that it took her several moments to regain her composure sufficiently to articulate her

thoughts. "Calhoun?" was all she could get out. "Mackenzie Calhoun? *My* Mackenzie Calhoun?"

"Your Mackenzie Calhoun?" Jellico made no effort to keep the surprise out of his voice. "Commander, I'm well aware of the rumors regarding a history between you and Calhoun. Still, it's been my impression that it's been many years since he was *your* Mackenzie Calhoun."

"Yes, yes, God yes," she said quickly, having regretted the slip the moment she'd said it. "There's no feelings in that regard. None. There had been a . . . brief flirtation, I admit . . ."

"How brief?"

She drew herself up stiffly. "I don't believe that is necessarily your business, sir."

"Agreed. How brief?"

With a sigh she said, "Three years."

"That's not what I'd call brief, Commander," Jellico said doubtfully. Then he shrugged. "Well, it's not as if you were engaged. . . ." And then he saw her look. "You . . . weren't engaged to be married, were you? Well?"

Endeavoring to rally herself, Shelby said firmly, "Admiral, I am asking you to take my word for it that the past is squarely in the past. Furthermore, I feel I must inquire as to . . . that is, I'm curious as to the thinking behind . . ." She cleared her throat, and then forced herself to remember her place and station in life. "Permission to—"

"Yes, yes, speak freely," said Jellico impatiently.

At which point Shelby promptly tossed aside any attempt to speak in a diplomatic or tactful manner. *"Dammit, Admiral, what the hell is going* on *in*

Starfleet?" demanded Shelby, the fury practically exploding out of every pore.

"I didn't quite mean *that* freely. . . ."

She didn't hear his dry response. She was too angry, waving her arms so vigorously that she looked as if she might go airborne any moment. "Putting aside that the *Excalibur* should be my ship . . . putting aside that I should have received my own command ages ago . . . putting aside all that . . . I find it personally infuriating that preference is being given to a man who walked away from Starfleet over an officer who has served unwaveringly and unstintingly!"

"I see you're determined to make this about you."

"Frankly, sir, since I'm the only one here aside from you, I think it's a thing for me to do." She shook her head. "May I ask whose decision this was? I know perfectly well it wasn't yours."

"Picard suggested it. . . ."

She rolled her eyes. "I might have known. Payback. Payback because I gave Riker a rough time."

Even though he knew it wasn't exactly the appropriate time, Jellico couldn't help but smile slightly. "Believe it or not, Commander, the galaxy doesn't revolve around you. Situations occur, decisions are made, people are born, grow old, and die, all without having anything to do with Elizabeth Shelby."

"I'm sorry, sir."

"Don't apologize. At the rate you're going, someday maybe it *will* all revolve around you. The point is, although Picard suggested Calhoun, it was Admiral Nechayev who sealed the deal."

"Nechayev?" She was clearly surprised. "I thought

there was no love lost between Nechayev and Picard."

"The last time I checked, there wasn't. There's something else going on, though. Something I haven't been able to completely find out about." He drummed his fingers on the desk thoughtfully. "There've been rumors floating around."

"What kind of rumors?"

"Stories, really. For instance, shortly after he resigned from Starfleet, Calhoun was alleged to have gotten into a serious drinking match with some admiral, and made a wager involving the world of Zantos."

"Zantos." Shelby made a face. "Wasn't that the world where a survey party got caught by the natives years ago, and they took the leader of the party and cut off his, uhm . . ." She shifted uncomfortably. ". . . his . . ."

"Privileges," Jellico said judiciously. "That's the place, all right. Never let it be said that Starfleet can't take a hint. We've steered clear of Zantos since then. However, Zantos apparently also produces the best ale in the quadrant. Better than Romulan ale, and tougher to get. Apparently, on a bet, Calhoun snuck onto Zantos, acquired a case of ale, and hotfooted it off the planet with half the Zantos fleet on his ass."

In spite of herself, Shelby smiled. "That sounds like Calhoun, all right." Then she shook her head. "But I don't understand what that has to do with anything."

"Perhaps nothing." Jellico shrugged. "Perhaps everything. Someone with that sort of attitude and resourcefulness might have been of interest to Nechayev. She has her fingers in a variety of 'unofficial,' 'behind the scenes' pies." He saw that Shelby was looking at him blankly and he sighed impatiently. "Do I have to spell it out for you, Commander?"

"Are you saying that Calhoun may have been involved in some sort of . . . of under-the-table information gathering, sir?"

"It's possible, Commander. We live in a universe of possibilities. What it all boils down to," and he leaned forward on his desk, "is that Calhoun apparently has powerful backers. And those backers are inclined to give him the *Excalibur* and turn him loose in the former Thallonian Empire."

By this point Shelby had sat in a chair across from Jellico. But Jellico's final statement seemed, to her, to more or less finish off the meeting. She slapped her legs, rose, and said, "Well, Admiral . . . I appreciate your candor." Trying to keep her voice even, to battle back the disappointment, she continued, "I hope you will keep my service record in mind for potential future assignments in—"

"Sit down, Commander, we're not done."

"We're not?" She was genuinely confused, even as she obediently sat again. "With all due respect, I'm not certain what else there is to say."

"I may have been overruled in the matter of the captaincy," said Jellico, "but I can pull enough strings to jump you to the top of the list for first officer."

She stared at him for a long moment. Then a short, disbelieving laugh jumped out of her throat, followed by longer, sustained laughter. Jellico displayed remarkable patience as he waited for the mirth to subside. It didn't happen quickly. Finally she managed to compose herself enough to say, "You're joking. You're not serious."

"Commander," he said evenly, "I have a reputation for many things, but it has come to my attention that 'comedian' is not one of them. Do I *look* not serious?"

"It's ridiculous."

"Ridiculous why?"

"For starters, I'm not interested in the post. Second, Calhoun would never accept me. Third . . ."

"Not interested in the post? Commander, I shouldn't have to do a selling job here," said Jellico impatiently. "It's a first-officer post on a ship with which you already have some familiarity. A ship that is about to embark on a very high-profile mission which offers excellent opportunities. As first officer, you'd be taking point on any away mission . . ."

She snorted. "You don't know Mackenzie Calhoun very well, Admiral. If you think he's going to sit around on the bridge while I spearhead away teams . . ."

"It's the first officer's job to make damned sure that the CO doesn't thrust himself into those types of high-risk situations." He leaned back in his chair and looked at her with what seemed to be faint disappointment. "Are you telling me, Commander, that you would be incapable of riding herd on Mackenzie Calhoun? That his bootprints would be all over you every time you tried to do your duty as you see fit? Well. Well well well," and he shook his head. "I guess I overestimated you."

Jellico could practically feel the waves of barely contained anger radiating from Shelby. "I did not say that, Admiral."

"I beg your pardon, Commander, but you most certainly did. . . ."

"I said Calhoun wouldn't sit still for it. That doesn't mean that I would just knuckle under." She smiled thinly. "To a certain extent, that's why we broke it off years ago. I wasn't his image of what he wanted in an ideal woman. I didn't jump to his tune, and I wasn't willing to make my career secondary to his."

"What a very old-fashioned attitude."

"He can't help it. It's part of his upbringing. When all is said and done, Xenexians aren't the most socially advanced of races."

"That is exactly my concern, Commander. Calhoun is a tricky devil. Very resourceful and very sneaky. I think he's going to need a first officer who knows all his tricks. Someone he can't pull any fast ones on, or try to steamroll over. Someone who can stand up to him." He permitted a small smile. "I'm not stupid, Shelby, nor am I completely disconnected. I knew damned well before you set foot in here that you and Calhoun had history together. In my opinion, that's exactly what he needs. And you have other . . . positives . . . that I think contribute to your viability as candidate for first officer."

"Those positives being that I'm ambitious," said Shelby. "That I want my own command. That if Calhoun screws up, I'm going to be there to note down the screwup in every detail so that, with any luck, we can get him out of the captain's chair and replace him with someone who deserves the position."

Jellico nodded. "I'm glad to see we're on the same wavelength, Commander. With your permission, then, I will put forward your application with my strongest recommendation."

She considered it for a long moment. "You do realize that he'll never go for it."

"Perhaps. Perhaps not. If I need to narrow the options available to him, I can pull a few strings in that department. I wouldn't do that immediately, of course; only if he proves 'reluctant.'"

"Ah. Well." She folded her arms and looked squarely at Jellico. "There's two other things that I think I should clarify, Admiral. The first is, reverse psychology is a fairly obvious tactic, and I wish you had not had to resort to it."

"Mmm-hmm," he said noncommittally. "And the second . . . ?"

"The second is," and she leaned forward with her knuckles on the desk, "if I should get the assignment, understand: My loyalty as first officer will be to my captain. It doesn't matter if we were once lovers. It doesn't matter if I think he's pigheaded, or stubborn, or a first-rate pain in the ass. If I sign on, I sign on for the entire package. I accept it and I deal with it. And if you think that I'm going to weasel my way on board and then turn around and be some sort of snitch, spy, quisling, rat, or in some other way, shape, or form search out means by which I can undercut or disenfranchise my superior officer, all for the purpose of advancement, then you, Admiral, with all due respect, can go screw yourself." And with that she turned on her heel and walked out the door.

Jellico sat there, staring at the space which she'd just vacated with undisguised amazement. And then, to no one in particular, he said, "Just once I'd like it if someone coupled the phrase 'with all due respect' with some sort of sentiment that was genuinely respectful."

SI CWAN

II.

SOLETA HAD BEEN CAUGHT completely flat-footed . . . a condition that was, to her, extremely annoying.

She was standing in her apartment in San Francisco. Her marvelous view of Starfleet Academy out the window had always provided a curious comfort for the Vulcan woman. Now it seemed to serve only as a sort of ironic counterpoint; out there would be possible rescue for her current odd situation, but it might as well have been on Venus.

On her computer screen, the words "Don't Move" . . . a message which had seemed very odd indeed when she first read it . . . still glowed at her in dark letters. "What kind of message is that?" she had demanded of the empty room.

That was when she had learned that the room was, in fact, anything but empty. From directly behind her, she'd felt the gentle but disturbing firm prodding of a weapon, and coldly spoken words: "It is the kind of message," a soft but threatening voice said, "that you should pay attention to, if you know what is best for you. Now . . . you shall do exactly what I say . . . and may God help you if you do not, because no one else will be able to help you. That, I can assure you."

Soleta was too well trained to let her astonishment show in either her voice or her demeanor. She acted, in fact, as if the identity of her unknown visitor were of no interest to her at all. "I am impressed," she said. "My hearing has always been rather keen. That you were able to gain access to this apartment and hide in here without my detecting you is, as noted, impressive. That you were able to then get close enough to me to threaten me with a weapon, again without my hearing your movement, is nothing short of amazing," and then, as an afterthought, she added, "which would have more impact, of course, were I capable of being amazed."

"You are unafraid," said the voice. "You have not changed."

The voice struck a cord in Soleta's memory. She frowned almost imperceptibly. "We have met, have we not."

"Think of an opulent corridor," the voice told her, almost seeming to relish prolonging the moment. "Think of an escape attempt gone awry . . ."

"On Thallon," she said slowly.

"Correct."

"Si Cwan."

As if saying the name somehow released her from

24

the threat of impending violence, Soleta turned to face him. Towering over her was indeed the formidable Lord Si Cwan, late of the Thallonian Empire. He had taken two steps back, clearly a respectful distance. "Stay where you are," he said firmly. "I am not interested in leaving myself vulnerable to the assorted Vulcan tricks at your disposal."

"Nor am I interested in utilizing them," replied Soleta, eyeing him with undisguised curiosity. "I still do not understand how I was unable to hear you come up behind me."

He shrugged as if it were an insignificant matter. "It is a technique I once learned. It is convenient for one who is as conspicuous as I to be able to blend in when such is required. I had a good teacher."

"I should say so." She gestured to a nearby chair. "Would you care to sit?"

Waving the barrel of his weapon slightly, he indicated another chair a few feet away. "After you," he said with exaggerated cordiality.

She nodded slightly and sat. A moment later he followed suit.

"The last time I saw you," said Si Cwan as casually as if they'd run into each other at a local pub, "you and Ambassador Spock were endeavoring to escape from Thallon. You'd staged a rather impressive breakout from your cell and were hoping to flee the palace when we happened to run into each other. Do you recall what happened?"

"Of course," she said. "You allowed the ambassador and myself to depart . . . after returning this to me," and she tapped the IDIC pin she wore in her hair.

He nodded. "All this time and you still wear it. It is comforting to know that some things in this ever-evolving universe remain unchanging."

"What happened after our escape?"

"Guards were disciplined. Palace security was improved. Drills were held."

"Nothing more . . . severe?"

"If what you are asking is if anyone was executed over their inability to keep you prisoner, no," Si Cwan assured her. "After all, the fundamental truth is that I allowed you to escape. Had I not done so, you would not have done so. It was a private decision I made, and one that I elected to keep private even as the investigation of your breakout was held."

"Why? You were a nobleman. Certainly you weren't afraid of retribution."

"Even noblemen have no desire to appear weak to their subordinates. It increases the difficulty of maintaining control."

"And yet," Soleta said evenly, "you lost control anyway. Your family lost control of the Thallonian Empire."

"A valid point," he admitted. "And, in fact, the reason that I am here." He seemed to regard her with intense interest for a moment, and then abruptly he holstered his blaster and placed his hands in his lap. The meaning of the gesture was unmistakable: It was time to put threats and attempts at intimidation aside. To be candid with, and trusting of, one another, if such a thing was possible.

"There are other things in this ever-evolving universe that should also remain unchanging, I should think," Si Cwan told her. "One of those is gratitude. Gratitude and appreciation for services provided, particularly when those services result in prolonging one's life."

"I would assume you are referring to the fact that I am indebted to you for having allowed me to escape Thallon."

"I am indeed."

She looked down for a moment, and there was a slightly rueful expression on her face. "Were I fully Vulcan," she said, "my attitude would be that, in allowing my departure, you acted in a most illogical manner. Behaving illogically would have been your prerogative as a non-Vulcan. Once you had decided to behave in an illogical manner, however, my attitude toward you would have been one of . . ." She paused, searching for the right word. "Contempt, I should think. Contempt and even a bit of fascination that one could achieve a position of power while pursuing such illogical thought patterns. 'Gratitude' would never enter into it."

He nodded grimly. "That would explain Ambassador Spock's attitude. I appealed to his sense of gratitude during a private meeting, asking him to do my bidding. He refused, and even seemed puzzled as to what I was talking about when it came to feeling obligated to me."

"Ambassador Spock is likewise not fully Vulcan. However, he has had far more time to come to terms with that fact and compensate for it. Out of curiosity, did you threaten him with a weapon as you did me?"

"No," he admitted. "I decided to utilize it this

time around for the purpose of emphasis." He considered the situation a moment. "May I take it from what you just said that you are *not* fully Vulcan? What are you?"

She fixed him with a level gaze and then said, with a softness that almost hinted at vulnerability, "I would prefer not to discuss it." There was silence for a moment, and then she said, "What did you want of Spock? For that matter, what do you want of me?"

"I need to get aboard the *Excalibur*. I need to be brought along, back into Thallonian space. It is important to me and, furthermore, I can be of use to you."

"You have already put in this request with Star-fleet, I take it."

"Yes, and I was denied. They denied . . . *me,*" and it was clear that the thought still rankled him.

"Why?"

"Because they are fools. Because I am not a member of Starfleet. One man, a man named Jellico, forbade it, and the others would not gainsay him. They united against me."

"And what would you have me do?"

"Get me onto the ship."

She stroked her chin thoughtfully. "I do not know the captain," she said, "but I can certainly speak with him once I am there. Arrange a meeting be-tween the two of you . . ."

"I am tired of meetings," Si Cwan said angrily. He rose from the chair, pacing furiously. "I am tired of groveling, tired of begging over matters that should be accorded to me out of a sense of correctness, of respect."

"Are you expecting me to sneak you on board somehow?" she asked skeptically.

And Soleta was completely unable to hide her astonishment when he replied, "Yes. That is exactly what I expect you to do."

"How? You're not exactly a Nanite, Si Cwan. You're over six feet tall. How would you suggest I smuggle you aboard? Fold you in half and put you in my suitcase?"

"I leave that to you and your resourcefulness."

"But if we speak to the captain . . ."

"He could say no. He very likely will. I expect that he will march in lockstep with his Starfleet associates."

"Even if I could somehow get you on board without anyone knowing," she said doubtfully, "you couldn't hide indefinitely."

"I'm aware of that. Once we're in Thallonian space, I'd make my presence known to your captain. By that point, it will be too late."

"Ship captains are historically not especially generous when it comes to stowaways, Si Cwan. In extreme cases, the captain would be authorized to punt you out of the ship in an escape pod with a homing beacon and no further obligation to see to your welfare. And since the captain is the one who defines what constitutes 'extreme,' he'd have a lot of latitude."

"I would deal with it."

"This is not a logical plan, Si Cwan. If you truly wish to go back into Thallonian space, you can hire a private vessel. As you well know, Sector 221-G is no longer forbidden territory."

"It is to some."

She raised an eyebrow. "Meaning?"

He dropped back into the chair opposite her, and with barely controlled anger, he said, "Understand me, Soleta. I still have followers. Many followers. At the risk of sounding self-aggrandizing . . ."

"A risk I'm sure you'll take," Soleta said dryly.

If he picked up on the sarcasm, he didn't let it show. ". . . I was one of the most popular members of the royal family. The mercy I showed you and Spock was not an isolated case. I helped out others from time to time, when such judicious displays could be performed without undue attention. In certain quarters, I was known as compassionate and fair, a reputation that was, quite frankly, deserved."

"My congratulations."

"By the same token, I also had enemies. One in particular, a man named Zoran, was almost insane in his hatred for me. I never knew quite why; only that Zoran would have done anything to see myself and the rest of my family wiped out. In any event . . . there were supporters who helped me and other members of my family to escape when the empire collapsed. And we were . . ."

His voice trailed off, as if he was recalling matters that he would rather not be thinking about. Soleta waited patiently.

"We were supposed to meet at a rendezvous point," he continued moments later, as if he hadn't lapsed into silence. "Meet there and get out together. I was the only one to make it to the rendezvous point. I heard secondhand that most of the others were caught and executed."

"Most?"

The entire time she had been watching him, he had maintained an imperious demeanor. But now it almost seemed as if he were deflating slightly. A great sailing ship, becalmed, its mighty canvas sagging. "I have heard nothing of Kallinda."

She was about to ask who that was, but then she remembered something. She remembered when she first met Si Cwan, seen him sitting on his mount, proud and regal. And next to him was a young girl, laughing, clearly adoring the man next to her.

"The little girl who was with you?" she asked. "When I was first caught?"

"Yes. My sister. My little sister, who never did harm to anyone. Who was filled with joy and laughter." He looked at Soleta, his dark eyes twin pools of sadness. "Kallinda. I called her Kally. I have been unable to determine what happened to her. I don't know whether she is alive and in hiding, or . . ."

As if he was suddenly aware of, and self-conscious over, his emotional vulnerability, he pulled himself together quickly. He drew his regal bearing around him like a cloak. "It is galling to admit, but I need the protection that only a starship can provide. Protection from enemies such as Zoran. The influence such a vessel could provide. And a means through which I can search for my sister. None of these could be garnered through the hiring of some small, one- or two-man ship."

"Lord Si Cwan, I wish I could help you, but . . ."

"No," he said sharply. "There will be no 'but's in this matter. I have need of your help, and you will help me. Once we are in Thallonian space I will more than prove my worth, but I need your assistance in getting me there. You owe me your life, Soleta. Not all the logical arguments, all the rationalizations in the world, are going to change that simple fact. If it were not for me, you would be dead; some rotting corpse in an unmarked Thallonian grave. If you have a shred of honor, you will acknowledge your indebtedness to me and do as I ask."

"I would be putting everything at risk, Si Cwan," she warned him. "If my complicity in such an endeavor were discovered . . ."

"It would not be discovered through me," he told her in no uncertain terms. "That much, at the very least, I can promise you. Do not take this wrong, but you would be merely a means to an end. But you are a means I must take advantage of, for I see no other way at this point. I cannot command you to help me, obviously. But I ask you now, for the sake of your own life, which you owe me . . . for the sake of my sister's life, which might possibly yet be saved . . . help me." And then he added a word that he could not recall using at any time in his life.

"Please."

And from the depths of her soul, Soleta let out a long, unsteady sigh, and wondered just who she should get to represent her at her court-martial.

III.

CALHOUN GLANCED UP from the computer screen as the door to his ready room slid open. Dr. Selar entered and, with no preamble whatsoever, said, "Dr. Maxwell's performance is unacceptable. Please dismiss him from the crew complement immediately."

"Computer off," said Calhoun as he rose from behind his desk. He gestured for Selar to sit. The Vulcan doctor merely stood there and, with a mental shrug, Calhoun sat back down again. "His performance is unacceptable?"

"That is correct."

"Did you have sex with him?"

Selar seemed taken aback, although naturally she did not let her surprise become reflected in anything more than a raised eyebrow. "I beg your pardon?"

"Did you have sex with Dr. Maxwell?"

"No, of course not. Nor do I—"

"Is Dr. Maxwell an actor? Does he tend to burst into monologues or soliloquies?"

Selar was completely lost. "Not to my knowledge. I do not see how—"

"Does he play a musical instrument?"

Giving up trying to understand where her captain was going with the conversation, Selar said simply, "It does not appear on his resume. If he does, he has not done so in my presence."

"Well, I was wondering. You see, you come in here complaining about his performance, and since I know perfectly well that no patients have come through sickbay yet, I assumed you couldn't possibly have evaluated his performance as a doctor . . . which is, last time I checked, the reason he was here."

She tilted her head slightly. "Captain Calhoun, are you always this circumloquacious?"

"No, not really. Generally I simply tell people whom I feel are wasting my time to get the hell out of my office. But we haven't even left drydock yet, so I'm trying to be generous." He came around the desk. "Look, Selar . . ."

"I prefer *Doctor* Selar."

He smiled. "I heard a joke once. What do you call the person who graduates at the bottom of their medical class?" Without waiting for her to respond, he answered, " '*Doctor.*' "

She stared at him.

"Do you get what I'm saying?" he asked.

"I believe so. You seek to diminish the title to

which I am due, based upon years of study and work, by implying that quality of scholarship may not be reflected in that title."

He rubbed his temple with his fingers and tried to remember why in God's name he'd let Picard talk him into this. "Look, Dr. Selar, it's your sickbay. If you want Maxwell out, he's out. I'm not going to argue. Perhaps you've perceived some potential trouble spots, or perhaps it's simply a personality clash. . . ."

"Vulcans do not 'clash,'" she informed him.

Keeping his voice even and calm, Calhoun said, "All I'm saying is that *you* are in charge of sickbay. The lineup for everyone working under you came from the Starfleet surgeon general's office. I okayed it based upon their recommendation, and I leave it to you to fine-tune it. Maxwell works under you. Use him, don't use him, blow him out a photon-torpedo tube for all I care. But I'll tell you right now, any changes in personnel have to be followed up with a formal report. I cannot put sufficient emphasis on this: I care very much about reports and following procedure. And you damned well better be ready to give concrete explanations for Maxwell's termination, because I think you should know that 'I felt like it' doesn't fly with Starfleet Central."

"I see."

"Now, if you want my recommendation—and the joy of being captain is that you get my recommendation whether you want it or not—I suggest you sit down and speak with Maxwell about those areas in which you find him lacking. See if you can come to some sort of accord. That would be something that I'd very much like to see."

"Are you offering your services as mediator, Captain, in order to facilitate matters?"

"Good God, no. I'd sooner stick my head in a warp coil. To be blunt, it sounds to me as if you're reacting out of some sort of core irrationality . . . which would be, to say the least, disturbing, considering who you are. Now, do your damn job and I'll do mine, and we'll both be happy. Or at least I'll be happy and you'll be," he gestured vaguely, "you'll be whatever Vulcans are. Now get the hell out of my office."

She headed for the door, stopping only to say, "You use more profanity than any other Starfleet officer I have encountered."

And with a wry smile, Calhoun replied, "I'm an officer. I'm just not a gentleman."

Burgoyne 172 was working with Ensign Yates, overseeing the recalibrating of the Heisenberg compensators in Transporter Room D when the signal beeped on hish comm badge. S/he rose quickly, narrowly avoiding bumping hish head on the underside of the control.

The Hermat was of medium build, quite slender and small-busted. S/he had a high forehead, pale blond eyebrows, and two-toned pale blond hair that s/he wore in a buzz cut, but that was long in the back. S/he tapped hish comm badge and said, "This is Burgoyne. Go ahead."

"Burgoyne? This is Shelby."

"Commander!" Burgoyne was genuinely pleased. S/he'd always gotten on well with Shelby, having worked with her on the *Excalibur* during the captaincy of the late, lamented Captain Korsmo. "How are you? For that matter, where are you?"

"I'm on a shuttle approaching drydock. They were kind enough to route this message through from the bridge. Tell me, Burgy, how long would it take you to get to a transporter room?"

Burgoyne smiled, displaying hish slightly extended canine teeth. "Well, let's see . . . allowing for the size of the ship, the measurement of my stride, the—"

"Burgoyne . . ."

"I'm *in* a transporter room, Commander, as it so happens."

"Perfect. I was hoping you could beam me aboard."

"That's against regulations." Burgoyne frowned. "Why not just dock in the shuttlebay? I'll inform the captain to meet you and—"

"That's what I was hoping to avoid."

"Avoid? I'm not following, Commander."

"I wanted to meet with the captain privately before I met with him publicly, if you catch my drift."

"I guess I do. You want to surprise him."

"In a manner of speaking. It'll be on my authority. Any problems with that?"

"None whatsoever, Commander. You're still technically my first officer until we leave port. If it's what you want, that's good enough for me. Just give me a moment to lock on to your signal," and hish long, tapered fingers fairly flew over the transporter controls, "and we'll bring you right on board."

Moments later the transporter beams flared to life, and Shelby appeared on the pad. She stepped down and stuck out a hand, which Burgoyne shook in hish customary extremely firm manner . . . so firm, in fact, that Shelby had to quietly move her fingers around in hopes of restoring circulation. "Good to see you, Commander."

"And you too, Lieutenant Commander."

"Shall I have Yates escort you to the bridge?"

"Oh, I think I can find the way."

And as she headed for the door, Burgoyne asked, "Are you going to be staying with us awhile, Commander?"

"That," said Shelby, "is what I'm going to try and find out."

Shelby stepped out onto the bridge and nearly walked straight into a mountain range.

At least, that's what it seemed like. She stopped dead in her tracks. She didn't really have much choice in the matter; her path was blocked. She looked up, and up.

The being who faced her was powerful and muscled, his skin a dusky brown with ebony highlights. Either one of his arms was bigger than both of hers put together, and he had three fingers on each hand: Two of the fingers in a [V]-shape, rounded out with an opposable thumb. His (assuming it was a he) head was squared off, like a rough diamond, and he had small earholes on either side of his skull. His nose consisted of nothing more than two vertical, parallel slits between his eyes that ran to just above his mouth.

"You've *got* to be a Brikar." She'd never seen one of the gargantuan beings before, but she'd heard them described. If what she'd learned about them was true, this behemoth could withstand phaser blasts that would kill a human . . . hell, kill a squad of humans.

He was wearing a Starfleet uniform that seemed stretched to its maximum, and all she could think was *Thank God he's on our side.*

"And you are?" he rumbled. His voice seemed to originate from somewhere around his boots.

"Commander Shelby. I'm here to see Captain Calhoun."

"I was not aware of your arrival, Commander."

"It's," and she bobbed her head from side to side slightly, "it's a bit of a surprise."

"I, with all due respect, sir, don't like surprises."

"Let me guess. You're in charge of security."

His eyes glittered down at her. She had a feeling he was eyeballing her quickly to see if she had weapons hidden on her. Apparently satisfied, at least for the moment, he said, "Wait here, Commander." The Brikar moved off toward the captain's ready room and entered. Shelby mused that it was fortunate the door opened fast enough. Otherwise the Brikar would likely have just walked right through it.

"Commander Shelby?" Shelby turned to see a pert young woman with a round face and dark blond hair, piled high on her head, standing near her. She had her hand extended and Shelby shook it firmly. "Lieutenant Robin Lefler. Ops. Burgoyne told me you were on your way up."

"I wish s/he'd told the walking landmass over there." She chucked a thumb in the direction that the Brikar had just gone.

"Wouldn't have mattered even if s/he had," said Lefler. "Zak is pretty single-minded. If the word doesn't come down from the captain, then as far as he's concerned, the word isn't given."

"Zak?"

"Zak Kebron. He's quite a piece of work, Zak is. I helped outfit him with a small gravity compensator he wears on his belt. The Brikar are such a heavy-gravity race that, if he doesn't wear the compensator, it makes it almost impossible for him to move. As it is, if he's in a hurry, you can hear him running from three decks away."

"I'd believe it."

"We have a few holdovers from when Captain Korsmo was in charge," continued Lefler. "They all had nothing but good things to say about you."

With a slightly mischievous air, Shelby said, "Well, they know better than to say anything bad."

Then Shelby heard a soft, rhythmic snoring noise. She looked for the source . . . and couldn't quite believe it. There was a lieutenant sitting at navigation, his feet propped up on the controls. His arms were folded across his chest, his head rising and falling with the rhythm of his snoring. He had short-cropped red hair and—curiously—freckles. Curious because Starfleet officers, not being exposed to tremendous amounts of sunlight in their insular adult lives, tended to be fairly freckle-free. Shelby turned to Lefler, an unspoken question on her face.

"He knows his stuff," Lefler said optimistically. "Really."

The door to the ready room slid open and Zak Kebron was standing there. "The captain will see you, sir," he said in a voice that sounded like the beginnings of an avalanche.

Shelby nodded briskly and headed into the ready room. Kebron stepped aside, allowing her to pass. The door slid shut behind him and Zak walked over to his station. Robin sidled over to Kebron and leaned over the railing. "Did the captain have any kind of reaction?"

" 'Reaction?' " He looked at her blankly.

"When he found out that the commander was here."

"Should he have?"

"I'm not sure. I was getting the impression that she was expecting . . ." Her voice trailed off. "I'm not sure what she was expecting. That's why I was asking you."

His face was immobile.

"Come on, Kebron. Did he smile? Frown? Did he seem tense, curious, excited, tepid . . . stop me when I hit a word that's accurate."

Nothing. Zak Kebron simply stared at her.

Lefler grunted in annoyance. "Lefler's newest law: Getting information out of you is like interrogating a statue." She turned away from him.

"Good," muttered Kebron.

* * *

Dr. Selar entered sickbay and went straight to her office. But she quickly became aware that Dr. Maxwell was following her with his gaze. He'd known fully well that Selar had been dissatisfied with his prep work in sickbay, and he had been perfectly candid about the fact that he thought Selar was being too hard on him. He had suspected, correctly, that Selar had gone to the captain to discuss the situation.

Unaccustomed to subterfuge, Selar turned and met his look squarely. And, in some ways, she felt as if she was looking at him—really looking at him—for the first time.

And she had never realized before how, with his dark hair, his squared-off jaw, his serious demeanor, Maxwell bore a passing resemblance to her late husband. To Voltak, who had died of a heart attack in the throes of *Pon farr.* Died while Selar had lain there helplessly, unable to aid him.

And the rational part of Selar's mind said, *No. That is ridiculous. Pop psychology, pat and unsatisfying. Having a negative reaction to a coworker because of a passing resemblance to Voltak? It is absurd. It is not logical. That cannot be it. There must be . . . other concerns.*

Except at that moment she couldn't think of any.

Deciding to break the uneasy silence, Maxwell stepped forward and said, "Dr. Selar . . . I'd like to know if you'll still be requiring my services."

"Do you have duties to attend to?" she asked him.

"Well . . . yes . . . but . . ."

"Then I suggest you attend to them. Our intended

departure time has not been altered, and it behooves you to be prepared." And she turned and walked away to her office, leaving a confused but happy Maxwell behind.

The first thing that Shelby noticed was the short sword mounted on the wall. She stopped and stared at it. Calhoun seemed entranced by his computer screen, more than content to have Shelby speak first. She didn't let him down. "You still have it?"

He didn't even have to look up to see what she was referring to. "Of course."

"Mac, that sword laid your face open. It almost killed you. I'd hoped you'd outgrow the need to hold on to such things."

"It reminds me of the importance of keeping my guard up. As does this," and he tapped the scar. Then he turned in his chair to face her for the first time. "I can't say I'm surprised to see you, Commander."

"We're being formal, are we, Mac?"

"Yes."

Without missing a beat, she said, "Very well. Captain, I hope you will excuse my unannounced appearance, but I wish to discuss a matter of some urgency."

"You want to apply for the position of first officer."

"That is correct." She noticed her own picture staring out from the computer screen. Calhoun was reading up on her latest stats. "Since you are already in the process of reviewing my service rec—"

"Jellico told me not to use you."

She shook her head slightly as if trying to clear water from her ears. "Pardon?"

"I received a communiqué from Admiral Jellico. He told me you would be applying, and that he could not, in good conscience, recommend you for the post."

"I see." Shelby had assumed that Jellico would be backing her up. All right . . . if he wasn't going to, then fine. Calhoun couldn't possibly be aware of all the dynamics involved in—

"I assume one of two scenarios to be the case," said Calhoun, tilting his chair slightly back. "Either Jellico wanted you to spy on me, and you told him to go to hell, so that in a fit of pique he's trying to block the assignment. Or else he's hoping that you will, at the very least, make my life miserable . . . and by telling me not to use you, he hoped to employ a sort of reverse psychology. Like in the old Earth story you once mentioned to me, about the rabbit begging not to be thrown into the briar patch, he figured that by telling me not to use you, I would then turn around and do so." He gazed at her blandly. "How would you assess the situation, Commander?"

She did everything she could to fight down her astonishment. For a moment she felt as if she were clutching on to a roller coaster, and couldn't quite understand why the sensation had a familiar feeling to it. Then she realized: She'd oftentimes felt like that during her relationship with Calhoun. *Why am I letting myself in for this again? I must be insane!* Those were the thoughts that went through her head.

All she said, however, was "I would . . . concur with your assessment, Captain."

"Good."

She cleared her throat. "Captain," she began, "there are some things you should know. . . ."

"I don't need to hear it, Commander."

"Sir, with all respect, I believe you do. My record has been exemplary, I have served as first officer on the *Excalibur*, on the *Enterprise*, on the—"

"I said I don't need to hear it."

"I'm the right person for this job and, to be blunt, I'm the right person for *your* job, but at the very least I can provide a valuable—"

"Commander," he said, his voice icy.

"If you'll just listen to me—!"

"Eppy, will you shut the hell up!"

Her back stiffened. "Yes, *sir.*"

"Much obliged, Eppy."

"However, I should point out that if I am not addressing you by your first name, it would likewise be appropriate if you were not to call me by that . . . annoying . . . nickname."

"Elizabeth Paul. E.P. Eppy."

"I remember the derivation, sir. I would just appreciate your not employing it."

"You didn't used to consider it annoying. You thought it affectionate."

"No, it always annoyed me. I was just reticent about saying so because of our . . . involvement . . . at the time."

He gave her a skeptical look. "You? Reticent?" He sighed and turned his back to her, swiveling his chair so that he was gazing out at the narrow sliver of starscape which was visible through the sides of drydock. "It was good seeing you again, Commander."

"And you, Captain. And I guess I should say . . . putting aside our history . . . that I wish you the best of luck in the reassumption of your career."

"I appreciate that. Where's your stuff?"

She stared in confusion at the back of his chair. "Stuff?"

"Possessions. Equipment. Gear. Did you bring it with you or are you sending for it? Don't tell me you're going to waste time going back for it."

"I don't understand . . ."

He sighed. "Commander, we have to be out of here in forty-eight hours. I need to know if we're going to be required to sit around and wait for you to retrieve your gear, or whether you can be ready to go by the time we're prepared to shove off."

"Are you saying you want me aboard the *Excalibur?*"

"Yes, that it what I am saying."

"In what capacity?"

He turned to face her with a disbelieving expression. "Chief cook and bottle washer. Good God, Shelby, are you going to make me spell it out for you?"

"I think so, yes, sir."

"Very well." He stood and extended a hand. "Congratulations, Commander. You are the new first officer of the *Excalibur,* presuming you still want the job."

"Yes, I still want the job." She shook his hand

firmly, but then a cloud crossed her face. "We might face a problem, however."

"That being—?"

"Well, the paperwork for my appointment has to be run past Admiral Jellico. If he was genuinely trying to block me because of—for whatever reason—that could be a problem. Procedures do have to be followed, reports must be made, and—"

"Shelby, I cannot put sufficient emphasis on this: I don't give a damn about reports and following procedure. The decision is mine, and the decision is made."

"Very well, sir."

She paused, as if wanting to say something else, and it was fairly obvious to Calhoun. "Well? Something else on your mind, Commander?"

"Captain." She shifted uncomfortably in place. "Our relationship . . . it was a long time ago. I'm over you. Way over you. I need to know if you're over me. I need to know if you took me on because of our past involvement."

"No, Commander. I took you on in spite of it. Dismissed."

"I just wanted to say—"

"Dismissed."

She nodded curtly, satisfied with the response, and walked out of the ready room. Calhoun turned back to his viewing port and stared out.

There had been any number of times when there had been people who thought he was crazy. The Danteri, for one, when he had led his people in revolt against them, thrusting himself into one dangerous situation after another with an abandon that many mistook for recklessness.

There had been fellow Starfleet cadets who were openly horrified, and secretly amused, by Calhoun's willingness to go toe-to-toe with the most formidable professors at the Academy, never hesitating to voice his opinion, never backing down if he was convinced that he was right.

In his sojourn on the *Grissom* he had learned the game of poker and quickly established a reputation as being capable of bluffing his way through any hand. Once they'd even brought in an empath as a ringer, and even the empath hadn't been able to get a bead on him.

The chances he had taken in subsequent years while performing the missions that Nechayev had liked to refer to as his "little adventures" on her behalf . . . well, Nechayev herself had said she thought he was out of his mind on more than one occasion, although that never stopped her from tapping him or his "peculiar skills" (as she termed them) whenever she needed something low-key handled.

But in all those times, in all those years of people thinking that he was crazy . . . never once had Mackenzie Calhoun himself shared that opinion about himself.

Until now.

"I just took on my former fiancée as my first officer," said Calhoun out loud. "I must be out of my mind."

"I assume she is qualified, sir."

The voice startled Calhoun, who swiveled around in his chair quickly to see a young Vulcan woman standing just inside the doorway. He mentally chided himself; he had been unforgivably sloppy. He'd actually been so lost in thought that he hadn't heard someone enter his ready room. In the old days back on Xenex, such carelessness could very likely have earned him a dagger lodged squarely in his back.

"Yes. She is eminently qualified, and that is all that matters," said Calhoun quickly. He stared at the Vulcan for a moment, her face familiar to him. Then it clicked: he'd seen it in computer personnel files. "You're Lieutenant Soleta."

"Yes, sir."

"Welcome aboard. We've been waiting for you."

"I encountered some . . . delays."

"I'd like to sit down with you and get a full picture of what you know of Thallonian space."

"As you wish, Captain. But first . . . there is a matter of some urgency that I need to discuss with you."

"Relating to . . . ?"

"My luggage."

He considered that for a moment. "Your luggage."

"Yes, sir."

He leaned forward, fingers interlaced, and said, "This should be good."

RYJAAN

IV.

"THIS IS NOT GOOD."

Ryjaan, the Danteri ambassador, had only recently returned to his homeworld. Now he stood in his opulent office, high above the capital city, looking out at his most impressive view. Far below him the people of Danter went about their business, unknowing and uncaring of the efforts to which Ryjaan and other government officials went for the purpose of preserving their safety.

"No, not good at all," he continued, and he turned to look at the person who was seated in his office. It was a Xenexian who bore a passing resemblance to another Xenexian once known as M'k'n'zy of Calhoun. The difference was that he was taller, and wider, and also considerably more well fed, to put it delicately. To put it indelicately, he was terribly out of shape. However, his hair was neatly trimmed, as were his fingernails. His clothes were extremely fancy, far more so than was common for any Xenexian. He was clad in deep purples, with high black boots and a sword dangling off his right hip. The sword was largely for ornamental purposes; the only time he drew it was to show it off for a young lady whom he might be trying to seduce. It was indeed impressive-looking; the fact that it had never been used in combat didn't detract from that.

"Your brother," Ryjaan continued, "could cause us serious problems, D'ndai."

D'ndai shook his head in slow disbelief. "They actually put him in charge of a starship?"

"I was unhappy about this starship business to begin with," Ryjaan said. "When I was at the meeting aboard the *Enterprise,* I hoped to head this matter off. It would have served our purposes quite well to have the Danteri be the most significant starfaring presence in . . . what did they call it . . . ?" He quickly consulted a report that he had produced after the meeting. "Ah, yes. On their charts, it's called Sector 221-G. My, the Federation has always had a knack for creative names, haven't they."

D'ndai said nothing. Somehow he didn't feel that his input was being urged. He was correct.

"So our interests have been preempted. Oh, certainly we can come and go as we please. But we will have to move stealthily. Subtly. We cannot make any overt moves at this time."

"That might be fortunate," D'ndai finally offered. "At a time when there is confusion and chaos, no one is certain whom to trust. The larger the presence, why . . . the larger the target."

"Indeed."

"Yes." He shrugged expansively. "Let the Federation come in with their huge vessel. Let them parade around and draw fire and attention from all quarters. And once they are gone . . ."

And then D'ndai was nearly startled out of his chair by the abrupt thud of a dagger slammed down into the desk. It had been driven into it with significant force by Ryjaan, and now it quivered there, a trembling metal representation of Ryjaan's anger. Yet his expression was extremely placid in contrast.

"That sounds very much to me, D'ndai, like some sort of contrived rationalization for a very unfortunate situation," said Ryjaan, his voice having taken on a dangerously silky tone. "As I mentioned before, your brother is the captain of the vessel."

"I don't understand how they could possibly have put him in charge."

"Nor do I. Nor am I interested in understanding, because ultimately whether we understand or not, it's not going to make a damned bit of difference. The question is, how do we deal with it. And the answer is simple: You are to talk him out of it."

"Me?"

"Who better? You're his big brother."

D'ndai shook his head. "You do not understand. It is rather . . . complicated."

Ryjaan studied him for a moment, and then said slowly, "D'ndai . . . we have had a long, healthy and mutually beneficial association these many years. I have helped you, you have helped me. We have taken a situation that could very easily have deteriorated into chaos and fashioned it into an equitable, beneficial situation for all concerned. Need I remind you that the continued growth and strength of the Danteri government is not only beneficial for Danter, but it also benefits your homeworld of Xenex? That being the case, I think you'd best explain to me just how, precisely, it is an overly complicated situation."

D'ndai slowly rose from his chair and began to circle the office. "You don't know what he's like," D'ndai told him. "You just don't."

"I don't follow. Are you saying—"

"I'm saying that he's incorruptible. That he has a strong sense of how things should be. And that he will pay little to no attention to my feelings on particular matters."

"But why? You were freedom fighters together. Fought side by side, won the liberation of your people from my government. Certainly he must feel some degree of indebtedness. Some sense of what the old days were like for you. It can't be that he simply doesn't give a damn about you."

"You don't know, you don't—"

D'ndai leaned against the glass of the window, his palms flat against it. He was struck by how cold the pane of glass was. "We fought for . . . ideals, Ryjaan. We fought for a certain view of how we wanted Xenex to be. And more than anything else, we fought for how we wanted to be. But once the basic freedoms for which we had fought so long and fiercely were finally won, things . . . changed."

"Changed how?"

"You know perfectly well how," D'ndai shot back, making no effort to hide the anger in his voice. "Once we won our freedom, we had to get down to the business of governing. M'k'n'zy, he discovered he had no taste for it. No interest in it. He left it to me to pull our fractured world together, went off on his damned fool career path toward Starfleet. And then he came back and he . . . he judged me." D'ndai felt his blood boiling with the humiliating recollection of it. "He came back to Xenex, all dressed up in that crisp new Starfleet uniform, and he looked down his nose at us. Like he was so much better than we. So much smarter, so much . . ." He fought to regain control of himself and only partly succeeded. "Nothing we had done was good enough for him. The government we had set up, the lives we had created for ourselves. He accused us of selling out our people to Danteri interests. He saw the lands we had garnered, the wealth we accrued that came as a result of doing business with your people . . . and it infuriated him."

"You did what you felt was right," Ryjaan said, not unsympathetically. "You did what *was* right. Treaties were signed, deals were made, understandings were entered into. Xenex is free, and everyone prospers."

"Not everyone. I prosper. Some of my peers and associates prosper. Others . . ."

"Others eke out livings, I grant you. But they didn't take the risks you did. You're a leader, D'ndai. You and your peers, all leaders." He walked around his desk and intercepted D'ndai, who was still pacing furiously. He clapped a hand on his shoulder. "Leaders earn more consideration, more rewards. Why else become a leader except to garner some special consideration?"

"That was always the difference with M'k'n'zy," said D'ndai bitterly. "He became a leader because the people needed a leader. The concept of accruing anything aside from danger and risk . . . it never occurred to him."

"And he's angry because it occurred to others." Ryjaan made a dismissive wave. "It is far more his problem than it is yours."

D'ndai heard the words, but somehow they did nothing to take the sting out of the recollections . . . recollections that he had thought he had long since managed to bury. M'k'n'zy, tall and straight and proud, looking contemptuously at D'ndai. Accusing him of selling out his people's interests, of becoming that which they had fought against. Telling him that Xenex was free in name only; that Danter had managed to sink its interests into Xenex in a far more insidious manner. And that this time, those who had fought for Xenex's freedom had virtually given it away again.

And all during that confrontation, D'ndai had barely said anything. He had withstood M'k'n'zy's tirade because, deep down, he had known it to be true. It had only been after his brother's departure that D'ndai had allowed his anger to build, had thought of everything he could have, or should have, said.

Ryjaan was silent for a brief time, and then he said, "However . . . even though it is his problem . . . it now becomes mine. I had hoped that I could count on you to control him."

"Ryjaan . . . if the entire Danterian government was not able to control him . . . what hope would I have?"

Ryjaan nodded thoughtfully. "A good point. But let us be blunt here, D'ndai," and his tone grew harsh. "We Danteri have, for the most part, been rather generous with you. We have asked little in return. As of this point, however, our interests are such that we need to ask a great deal. We need to ask you to exert whatever influence you have to convince your brother that our interests are his as well."

"And if I may be as equally blunt," replied D'ndai, "I don't think I have a prayer in hell of accomplishing that. I am curious, though, as to just what those Danterian interests might be. It would certainly help bring the larger picture into better perspective."

Ryjaan looked up toward the stars, as if he were capable of picking out the exact location of the Thallonian homeworld and fixing it with a gaze. "I have been candid with you thus far, D'ndai. I have no reason not to continue to be . . . do I?" He watched D'ndai's reaction, which amounted to nothing more than a strongly held poker face. "The planet Thallon," he continued, "in all of our most holy books, is a source of great power. The most learned and mystic of the Danteri elders call it the Rest World."

"Rest World? Why?"

"The reasons are somewhat lost to obscurity. It is our guess, however, that centuries ago, great fleets may have used the Thallon homeworld as some sort of a resting and refueling point. Why, we don't know. As I noted, it is merely conjecture. The point is, however, that we have waited a long, long time to have the opportunity to explore the secrets that Thallon possesses, whatever they might be. Perhaps some new source of limitless energy. Perhaps weaponry left behind by tremendously advanced races which could be of use to us. The possibilities are infinite . . . provided that the Danteri need not worry about interference from the Federation."

"From my understanding, it is the Starfleet mandate that there be no interference."

"Mandates are one thing. However, the simple fact is that we have to deal with a starship being captained by a Xenexian. A Xenexian, moreover, who was key in disrupting Danterian interests in the past, even when he was a know-nothing teenager. And he is quite far removed from that relatively lowly status. Now he is a knowledgeable adult with the power of a starship at his fingertips and the authority of the Federation covering his backside. If he desires to make life difficult for us, he can do so very, very easily. We will have to skulk about and proceed with extreme caution as it is, and that will be a major inconvenience. We wish to make certain that our inconveniences are limited to their current status. The fall of the Thallonian government is the ideal time for the Danteri to consolidate power. Your brother should not—*must not*—get in the way of that, both for his good and for our own. Are we clear on that?"

"Perfectly clear, Ryjaan. But I do not, as of yet, know exactly how to proceed."

"Then I suggest you find a way, D'ndai." He returned to his desk, sat behind it, and then in a great show of confidence which he didn't exactly feel, he brought his feet up and placed them on the desktop. "Because if you do not find a way, then we shall have to. And that would be most unfortunate for all concerned." He paused and then repeated for emphasis, *"Most* unfortunate."

Captain's Log, Stardate 50924.6. We have launched from drydock and are on course as ordered.

First Officer's Log, Stardate 50924.7. We have achieved launch from drydock with a minimum of difficulty, and are proceeding toward Sector 221-G at warp six. I noticed in the captain's public log that he did not, as is Starfleet custom, enter the text of his launch speech. The launch speech is a long-standing Starfleet tradition. Some ship commanders read a prepared text, and some even read the same text on whatever ship they helm. Captain Calhoun chose to speak extemporaneously. In the interest of historical completeness, I am hereby entering it into the official log of the Excalibur *via this entry. The speech was delivered via intraship audio at precisely 1120 hours on Stardate 50924.5:*

"Gentlemen . . . ladies . . . this is Captain Calhoun. I welcome you all aboard the Excalibur, and look forward to the adventure in which we have been . . . thrown together, for want of a better phrase.

"For many of you, this is your first time aboard a starship. It may seem vast, even intimidating to you at first. It is not. I would wager that our little populace of six hundred and three, in comparison to the cities in which you likely grew up, is rather small. Furthermore, when we are measured against the vastness of the void we are about to hurl ourselves into . . . we are barely more than a speck.

"I have followed a rather . . . roundabout path to becoming your captain. I'm sure you all have your own stories, your own histories, your own reasons for joining Starfleet. I'm telling you now: They are all irrelevant to the job at hand. In the days of old Earth, I am told, there was an organization called the Foreign Legion, which men of questionable backgrounds could join in hopes of starting new lives for themselves. In a way . . . you are starting new lives here. Who you are, what you may have accomplished before . . . these are the elements that led you here. But from now on, anything you do will be, first and foremost, as crewmen of the Excalibur. It is to that ship, to that name, and to your fellow crewmen, that I expect you to give your first allegiance.

"We are all we have. There are no families, no 'civilians' aboard the Excalibur. That is a luxury that I am afraid is left to larger vessels. Those of you who do not have families back home—and even those of you who do—look around you. The people to your left and right, behind you and in front of you . . . they

*are your family now. You will confide in them, depend
on them, laugh with them, love them, hate them, and
be willing to put your lives on the line for them.
Nothing less than that level of dedication will do,
because only under those circumstances will we be
able to survive . . . and more . . . to triumph.*

"All right. What are you all doing standing around,
listening to your captain chatter on as if he is saying
something you didn't already know. Back to work."

*Captain's Personal Log, Stardate 50924.7. Our
launch was proceeding perfectly well until my first
officer insisted I get on the loudspeaker and make a
fool of myself to the crew. I don't even remember what
I said: some sort of over-the-top, cloying, "Go get
them, boys and girls" oration. Damnation, is this
what modern-day Starfleet members need to bring
them together? It was much easier on Xenex. All I
needed to do was raise my sword over my head, shout
"Death to the Danteri!" and the huzzahs would roll.
Had I been wise, I would have informed Eppy that if
she wanted a speech, she could damned well make it.
But everyone looked to me as she stood on the bridge
and suggested it; I didn't wish to seem a coward. It
has been many years since I cared overmuch how I
seemed in the eyes of others, and it is a disconcerting
feeling. At the very least, I must take care to make
certain that Eppy not put me in that sort of position
again.*

*First Officer's Personal Log, Stardate 50924.7. The
captain made a stirring and moving speech upon
launch, which he would not have done had I not urged*

him into it. Although Calhoun's strategic skills and starship knowledge are indisputable, his people skills are in need of honing. It is my belief that, although Captain Calhoun has some rough spots to him, with my guidance he will develop into a thoroughly adequate leader. However, I do feel I need to discuss the contents of his off-the-cuff remarks, for the purpose of making certain that mixed messages are not sent to the crew.

V.

SI CWAN FLOATED in a point of consciousness between wakefulness and sleep. As he attained this state, his heart rate had slowed down to a point where it was almost undetectable. His breathing was incredibly shallow. He could have stayed that way indefinitely.

The darkness in the storage container was complete. But it did not bother him. He wasn't even aware of it.

In his semiconscious state, images floated in front of him. Images of his father, mother, uncles, all floated past him. All dead or missing, and even in his dreamlike haze, he didn't care overmuch. He had never liked most of them, had never gotten on with any of them. For they had tended to think of the Thallonian people as far beneath them, not only in their social status, but in their rights as sentient creatures. It was a philosophy that Si Cwan had never shared, and as a result he had gotten into any number of angry disputes over it. Although to the public they presented a united front, behind closed doors it was a very different story. Si Cwan had worked behind the scenes to get every consideration for the outlying regions of the Thallonian Empire.

And slowly, word had spread throughout the channels that such things always did. If there was a grievance to be filed, if there was a request to be made, it gradually became known that Lord Si Cwan was the one to make it through. For a time this had a beneficial effect, but soon word of Si Cwan's growing reputation reached the wrong ears in the palace. As a result, Si Cwan found every suggestion of his meeting with greater resistance than ever.

In the floating darkness of his semiconsciousness, Si Cwan saw himself arguing, warning, threatening. The fall of the Thallonian Empire was coming, any fool could see that. Why would they not open their eyes? Why would they not listen? But he could see the answer to that question in their faces. See the arrogance, the overwhelming self-confidence which would cost them dearly in the long run.

And there *she* was. There was Kallinda. Her arms outstretched, her face pleading, and in his mind's eyes she was mouthing the words *Help me.* Damn him for being off-planet when the trouble started. He, who had seen it coming, was in the wrong place at the wrong time. Of course, some would say that when an empire is collapsing, not being in the thick of it was the best position for someone at risk. But Si

Cwan had precisely the opposite sentiment. If he had been there, he might have saved those close to him. Or, worst came to worst, he would have died with them.

Instead he now felt as if he were in limbo, floating, floating . . .

. . . floating . . .

And suddenly, brutally, Si Cwan was dragged back to reality.

He was jolted out of his meditative haze, light flooding him from everywhere. Caught completely off guard, he had no time to mount a defense as he was lifted bodily out of his hiding place.

His "hiding place," in this instance, consisted of a shining silver crate which was situated in one of the secondary cargo bays of the *Starship Excalibur*. It was relatively small, the ostensible contents being "Foodstuffs." Because of its limited space, Si Cwan was practically forced to fold himself in half in order to fit.

Under ordinary circumstances, it should have been many minutes, if not hours, before Si Cwan could possibly offer any sort of physical protest. He had brought minimal food and water into the container with him, since space had been at a premium and he wasn't exactly able to pack bathroom facilities in with him; furthermore, he had been exceptionally judicious in its use since he had not been entirely certain when he was going to be getting out of his hiding place. He had spent most of the time carefully regulating his bodily requirements, and as a result all the muscles in his body should have been completely slack. Furthermore his heartbeat had been slowed almost to nonexistence, and so getting adrenaline pumping so that he could attack should have been flatly impossible.

But circumstances, when it came to Si Cwan, were never ordinary.

As Si Cwan was being hauled out of the container, he barely had time to register the nature of his assailant. Whatever it was, it was a race unlike any that Si Cwan had ever seen before. His skin looked like thick, dark leather, and he was clutching Si Cwan with a massive three-fingered hand. He didn't know what this creature was capable of, and he didn't want to take the time to find out. Furthermore, despite the fact that he had stashed himself away in a very humble manner, he still possessed enough of his dignity to take umbrage at such treatment.

"I am *Excalibur* security chief Zak Kebron, and you are under—" Kebron began to say. And then Si Cwan's legs, which by all rights should have been immobile, lashed out. He drove both heels squarely into Kebron's face, staggering him by a grand total of an inch and a half. Kebron shook it off so quickly and easily that the blow might as well not have landed at all. "—arrest," he finished. There were several crewmen standing nearby, but all of them were general-maintenance crew. None of them were Security. Apparently Kebron considered himself all that was required to handle the present situation.

"Put me down," snarled Si Cwan, his feet dangling a meter above the ground.

"You are hardly in a position to bark orders," Kebron replied evenly. He seemed like someone who never lost his temper. It was entirely possible he never needed to.

Si Cwan, however, was not of similar temperament . . . particularly so considering the present situation. His body should have been unable to respond to the orders his brain was conveying, but through sheer force of will, Si Cwan struck back much faster than Kebron would have thought feasible.

His long legs scissored upward, and Si Cwan snagged Kebron's head firmly between his knees. Kebron staggered slightly, apparently more from confusion than from actual pain or even discomfort. And then, in an astounding display of physical control, Si Cwan twisted at the hip while in midair, achieving enough leverage to send Zak Kebron tumbling to the floor. At the last second Si Cwan leaped clear and Zak hit the ground with a sound and vibration not unlike that of an avalanche.

"I demand to see your captain!" Si Cwan announced as he scrambled to his feet.

Kebron did not seem in the mood for bargaining. "All you're going to see is the inside of the brig," he shot back as he clambered to his feet.

Si Cwan opted for discretion being the traditional better part of valor. For all he knew, the process of "due trial" on the *Excalibur* might be nothing more involved than this monstrous security guard unilaterally stashing him in a cell until he rotted. He had to find the captain. Certainly a man who lived his life in a position of command would be able to understand Si Cwan's predicament and accord him the courtesy to which his station in life entitled him.

It would have been impossible for any observer to guess that Si Cwan had been nearly paralyzed mere seconds before. He spun on his left heel, his right leg lashing out, and it squarely connected with the lower part of Kebron's face. A shuddering impact ran the length of his leg. It didn't manage to hurt Kebron any more than the first blow had, but it at least served to knock him off balance and send him down to the floor again. Si Cwan came to the quick and dismaying realization that, at least with matters the way they currently were, there was absolutely no way he was going to be able to defeat Kebron for any length of time. Kebron could afford to hit the floor. He could be knocked down a dozen times or more; it didn't matter. Because he would keep getting back up, as strong as ever and probably angrier each time.

Si Cwan bolted.

Two of the crewmen who had been watching the altercation tried to get in the way. Si Cwan leaped high, slammed out with both feet, and knocked them both flat. He landed lightly and was about to get out the door when it slid open moments before he got there. Someone else was about to enter.

Si Cwan didn't slow down, driving a fist forward so quickly that—to any onlooker—it would have been a blur.

And that was to be the last thing that Si Cwan remembered. That and a shouted word which sounded like, *"Later!"*

"Captain, a moment of your time, please," Shelby said as she spotted Calhoun exiting his quarters and heading toward the turbolift.

"Walk with me, Commander," he said briskly as he stepped into the lift. She followed him in, fully expecting that he was going to tell the lift to take them to the bridge. Instead he said, "Deck twelve."

"Deck twelve?" she said in mild surprise.

"Luggage problem," he replied. Her blank expression made clear that she had no idea what he was referring to, but before she could pursue it, he continued, "You have the moment of my time, Commander. What is it?"

"It's about your speech, sir. The 'welcome aboard' launch speech."

He nodded. "Brilliant oration, I thought."

"Yes, absolutely, there's just—"

"Just?" He eyed her skeptically. "Is there a problem?"

"Well, it was the part about the crew's first loyalty being to the ship and the ship's name and to each other."

"You disagree?"

"I don't dispute that those are important elements. But don't you agree that, first and foremost, loyalty should be to Starfleet and the ideals it teaches?"

He studied her levelly. "Of course," he said in a neutral manner. "Well-phrased. I agree, of course. Excuse me." The turbolift door slid open and Calhoun strode out, leaving Shelby behind. She was about to let the door slide closed when, with a frown, she ordered it to remain open and followed Calhoun out. He was walking with a brisk pace down the corridor and Shelby was hard-pressed to keep up, but she'd be damned if she asked him to slow down.

"With all respect, Captain, I believe I recognize that tone of voice."

"Do you?"

"Yes, I do. That's your I-don't-agree-but-I'll-say-anything-to-avoid-an-argument-I'll-probably-lose tone."

He didn't slow his stride, but a small smile did flicker across his lips. "I don't know that I'd concur with the 'probably lose' part, but the sentiment has merit."

"Captain, we are not going to be able to function if you do not tell me your state of mind at any given moment."

"Not my style, Commander."

"I'm sorry . . . what? Your *style?*"

Calhoun had stopped walking directly in front of the entrance to a cargo bay. He seemed to be listening carefully for something.

"Your style?" Shelby said again.

"Commander, later."

"Captain, I believe this indicates a larger issue that should be—"

The door suddenly slid open and a tall, dark red, and apparently very angry Thallonian intruder was barreling through it.

"I said later!" shouted Calhoun.

Calhoun seemed to register on the Thallonian's personal radar as nothing more than obstruction, something to be cleared out of the way as quickly and expeditiously as possible. Shelby, reacting in the proper procedure for such an emergency, slapped her comm unit and managed to get out, *"Shelby to Secur—!"* just as the Thallonian charged.

The captain moved so quickly that it seemed as if he weren't even hurrying. A quick step took him to the side of the Thallonian's path, and then Calhoun's right arm was a blur. His fist slammed into the side of the Thallonian's temple, striking a pressure point with such precision that the Thallonian was unconscious before he even fully realized it. His eyes disfocused and his hands clutched spasmodically at thin air. And then the Thallonian pitched forward and hit the floor. It seemed as if Calhoun were in a position to catch him, but the captain's arms remained securely at his sides as the Thallonian thudded to the floor.

The entire thing—the attack, the defense, and the dispatching of the opponent—had all occurred so rapidly that Shelby had barely finished the word with "—*ity* . . ." before the Thallonian was laid out in front of her.

Calhoun was staring down at the Thallonian with cool dispassion, and then Zak Kebron emerged from the cargo hold. "You called, Commander?" he rumbled.

"Quick response, Lieutenant," Calhoun said without missing a beat. "Well done."

"Thank you, sir," said Zak.

"If I am not mistaken," Calhoun continued, staring down at the prostrate form, "we are graced with the presence of Lord Si Cwan of the former Thallonian Empire. Lieutenant," and he gestured in Si Cwan's general direction.

Kebron reached down with one hand and picked the insensate Si Cwan off the ground. "Brig or sickbay, sir?"

"If we put him in sickbay, under the careful ministrations of Dr. Selar, he will likely wake up with no headache. In the brig, he'll wake up feeling like his head's going to fall off." He gave it a moment's thought. "Brig."

Kebron seemed to smile almost imperceptibly. "Good." And he proceeded to cart Si Cwan off down the corridor.

As he did so, Calhoun turned to face Shelby and smiled. "Now . . . you were saying?"

She looked at Kebron's departing form and then back to Calhoun. "You knew he was down here. You weren't coming here by coincidence. You knew perfectly well that that man, Si Cwan, was in the cargo hold."

"Yes."

Calhoun could see rage starting to build within Shelby, her body trembling in barely restrained fury. The door was just closing to the cargo bay when Shelby stormed through it. Calhoun followed her in, more out of curiosity than anything else.

The workers looked up as Shelby entered, but before any of them could say anything, Shelby snarled with barely contained fury, "All of you, out! Now!" Even under ordinary conditions they would not have been inclined to question an order, but considering Shelby's demeanor they were practically tripping over each other to evacuate the area. Shelby turned on her heel, smoldering, as Calhoun entered the cargo bay, the doors hissing shut behind him. Before he could get a word out, she turned and said with unbridled ire, *"How dare you? How* dare *you!"*

"Shouldn't you be asking for permission to speak freely?" he said, unperturbable.

"To Hell with that and to Hell with you, Mac! How *dare* you not inform me that you were aware we had an intruder on board! I'm your second-in-command! If I learn anything of importance then I inform you immediately, and I expect the same courtesy from you!"

"I'm afraid I can't agree. There will be times, Elizabeth," he replied in a formal tone, "when information will be on a need-to-know basis. And if, in my judgment, you don't need to know, then I can and will exercise discretion to keep that to myself."

Her flat hands swept the air in an impatient gesture. "Understood, of course, understood. But there is a line, Mac, between keeping things to yourself on the basis of Starfleet security, and keeping things to yourself out of some sort of misplaced need to prove yourself."

"I have no such need, Elizabeth, I assure you."

"Oh, bullshit," she snapped. He raised an eye at the profanity, but she steamrolled on. "You have plenty to prove. You walked out on Starfleet, carrying guilt with you for years, and now you're back with more responsibility than you've ever known, and you're out to prove that you can do it all. Captain Mackenzie Calhoun, the one-man band of the *Starship Excalibur*. Well, it doesn't work that way, Captain. Not on any ship that I've ever been on. You think you're Atlas, carrying the entire universe on your shoulders, and if anything on this ship goes wrong, it's your fault. It wasn't true on the *Grissom,* and it's not true here."

His face clouded. "Leave the *Grissom* out of this, Elizabeth. If you have something to say, say it and be done with it."

She looked down, the initial force of her fury spent, and then, still studying the floor, she told him, "All I'm saying is that part of being a team means that everyone has responsibility, even though you have the ultimate responsibility. But even though you have that ultimate responsibility, your priority still has to be functioning as part of that team. That's where your priority has to lie. That's where your first allegiance has to be. To the *Excalibur* and the people on . . . her . . ."

Her voice trailed off. He stared at her, a carefully maintained deadpan firmly in place, as he said, "Funny. I was saying that earlier and you were arguing with me about it. I'm glad you've come around to my way of thinking. If you'd care to join me at the brig . . . ?" And as he headed out of the cargo bay, the doors slid open to reveal the assorted crewmen who had vacated the bay moments earlier. They were trying to look nonchalant or otherwise occupied; in short, like anything except people who were eavesdropping. They quickly dispersed, leaving Shelby alone.

"I hate that man," she sighed.

HUFMIN

VI.

THE CAPTAIN OF THE *Cambon* didn't realize the danger until it was too late.

His name was Hufmin, he was a veteran star pilot and occasional smuggler from Comar IV, one of the worlds in the outer rim of the former Thallonian Empire. With many of his usual customers and routes in disarray, he was nevertheless turning a nice profit by offering his services to some of the more well-to-do refugees of the collapsing Sector 221-G. At least, that had been his intention. But somewhere along the way, as he had lent his aid for what had been intended as a mercenary endeavor, he had discovered—much to his annoyance—that he had a heretofore unknown streak of sentimentality. Perhaps it had been the desperate look of some of the women, or, even worse, the grateful faces of the children looking up at him. The *Cambon*'s comfortable complement was twenty-nine passengers; Hufmin crammed on forty-seven, many of them at less than the going rate and some of them—God help him—gratis. He considered it nothing short of a major weakness on his part. He could only hope for two things: that when this immediate crisis was over he would come to his senses, and that he did not suffer any misfortune, since he firmly believed that no good deed went unpunished.

With the *Cambon*'s facilities stretched beyond capacity, Hufmin decided to take a chance and cut through an area that was off his usual routes. On his starmaps it was listed as the Gauntlet, a holdover from more than a century ago when fleets from two neighboring worlds would take to the space between the worlds and blast away at each other. But that was long ago, and the area hadn't been a shooting gallery for ages. Granted, it had been the firm grip of the Thallonian Empire—to say nothing of the Thallonian's summary execution of the warring planetary heads as a warning to all concerned—that had brought a nominal peace to the area. And granted that, with the fall of the Thallonian Empire, anything could happen. But Hufmin couldn't believe that if the situation were to change, it could possibly happen fast enough to be a threat to his ship or its passengers.

He thought that for as long as it took for the first of the attack ships to drop out of warp.

He had gotten halfway through the Gauntlet when his sensors began screaming alarms at him from all sides. Frightened passengers began to call to him, asking what was going on, and all he could tell them to do was to shut up and buckle down. He couldn't believe what his sensors were telling him: attack vessels on both sides of him, all of them many times the size of Hufmin's modest transport, taking aim at each other. They didn't give a damn about him. They were only interested in blowing each other out of space.

Unfortunately, the *Cambon* was squarely in the way.

Hufmin banked furiously, slamming the controls forward, as the *Cambon* desperately tried to get clear of the area before the shooting started.

The vessels opened fire and suddenly the entire area of space was a hot zone. The ships fired with no particular grace or artistry, making no attempt to pinpoint respective targets and try for maximum damage with minimum fuss. Instead it was as if they were so overjoyed to have restraints removed from them that they simply let fly with everything they had. Blasts flew everywhere without regard for innocent bystanders. The attitude of the combatants was simple: Anyone who was within range should never have wandered in there in the first place.

The *Cambon* was hit twice amidships, and then a third time. The engines were blown completely off line, and only the laws of physics saved it, for the impact of the blasts sent the ship spiraling wildly. And since objects in motion tend to stay in motion, the *Cambon* was hurled out of immediate danger as the already existing speed of the ship carried it away from the firefight which had erupted in the Gauntlet.

Which did nothing to solve the *Cambon*'s long-term problems. Hufmin desperately tried to keep the ship on course, but failed completely. The ship was utterly out of control. Hufmin endeavored to concentrate on fixing the situation. But it was all he could do to focus on the problem at hand, for he had cracked his head fiercely on the control consoles when he was first hit. There was every likelihood that he was concussed. Indeed, he felt a distant blackness already trying to settle on him, and it was all he could do to fight it away.

He hit the autosend on the distress signal and prayed that someone would hear it. And then he vomited, uttered a quick prayer that they wouldn't fall into a sun, and slumped to the floor.

Out of control, unpiloted, and with apparently no hope in hell, the *Cambon* spiraled away into the void. Behind them two mighty fleets continued to shoot at each other, uncaring of the damage they had wrought. Without ten minutes the battle was over, as battles in space tend to end fairly quickly. The surviving ships limped back to their respective homes, and word was sent out that the Gauntlet was to be avoided at all costs.

Word that the *Cambon* would have been happy to spread . . . provided that anyone on it survived to spread it.

VII.

CALHOUN STOOD OUTSIDE the brig, his arms folded. Si Cwan was standing inside, rather than sitting. Calhoun hated to admit that he was somewhat impressed by this; he could tell from the semiglazed look in Si Cwan's eyes that the Thallonian was fighting off ripples of pain and residual dizziness. He could just as easily have been seated, but something about him—pride, determination, arrogance, stubbornness—prompted him to be on his feet.

"Feel free to sit," Calhoun invited.

"I wish to remain taller than you," replied Si Cwan.

Inwardly, Calhoun smiled. Outwardly, all he did was glance at Shelby, who was standing at his side for a reaction. She rolled her eyes in a manner that simply said, *Men*. Of course, that might have applied equally to Calhoun.

"I am Lord Si Cwan," Cwan said archly.

"Captain Mackenzie Calhoun. Would you care to tell me why you stowed away on my vessel?"

"How did you know I had done so?"

"I ask the questions here," Calhoun said sharply.

Unperturbed, Si Cwan replied, "As do I."

Zak Kebron was standing nearby, his massive, three-fingered hands on his hips, watching the questioning. "Shall I break him in half, sir?" he asked. There was no eagerness in his voice, nor trepidation. It was merely a matter-of-fact query.

Calhoun gave it a moment's thought. "Go ahead, Lieutenant. If nothing else, it'll cure him of his annoying standing."

Kebron nodded and reached for the button to deactivate the field so that he could enter the brig and fold Si Cwan backward. Shelby looked from the expressionless Calhoun to Kebron to Si Cwan, who looked slightly disconcerted by the abrupt direction that matters were taking. She turned so that her back was to Cwan as she whispered to Calhoun, *"Captain!* With all due respect, you can't do that!"

"I'm not," Calhoun said reasonably, making no effort to keep his voice down. "Lieutenant Kebron is. Lieutenant, go ahead. Break him in half. Or a sixty-forty split would suffice. This isn't an exact science."

Shelby stared intently into Calhoun's eyes . . . and then understanding seemed to dawn. She turned back to Si Cwan and said, "I tried. I tried to talk him out of it. He won't listen to me. If it's of any consolation, I'll be sending a stern report to Starfleet in regards to this heinous treatment. If you'll excuse me," and she started to walk away.

Kebron shut off the forcefield and stepped in, immense fists flexing.

"Wait!" Si Cwan said, taking an unsteady step backward. Then he cleared his throat, trying to regain his composure. "Wait," he repeated, far more calmly this time. "I see no reason that we need to be adversarial about this. I . . . need passage back to my system. Back to Thallonian space."

In quick, carefully chosen phrases, he laid out his situation for them. Who he was, his desire to turn home, his need for protection that only a starship could provide.

"And you felt that sneaking on board was preferable to simply approaching the captain directly?" asked Shelby.

"I had already broached the notion to his superiors," Si Cwan said. "They had refused me. To encourage a subordinate officer to take actions counter to the sentiment of his superiors—even though they were sentiments that angered me— would have been dishonorable."

"But that's what you're doing now, isn't it?" Shelby countered. "You're asking him to countermand those orders."

"I am already here," replied Si Cwan. "It is a different situation. I am giving him no choice *but* to countermand them and accept me as a passenger."

"So it's all right to force someone to help you, but

it's not all right to simply ask them," asked Shelby. Si Cwan made no reply, but merely gave a small shrug.

"What makes you think I won't toss you out of the ship right now? Leave you to fend for yourself? For that matter, what's to stop me from simply throwing you bodily out into space right now?" Calhoun asked. Shelby knew damned well that, for starters, Starfleet regulations would stop him. But she said nothing since she didn't want to undercut her captain . . . and besides, one never knew with Mackenzie Calhoun. Shelby was ninety-nine percent sure that he wouldn't take such an action, but it was the remaining one percent that made her hold her tongue.

Unaware of what was going through Shelby's mind, Si Cwan replied, "Because to do so would be a tremendous waste of material. One does not become a leader of men by wasting material and opportunities when they present themselves." Si Cwan looked and sounded utterly confident. Whether he genuinely was or else was simply putting on the act of his life, Calhoun wasn't entirely sure.

"And what purpose would you serve on my ship, may I ask?"

"Goodwill ambassador. A connection to what once was in the hope of building that which will be. A guide through areas of space which are unfamiliar to you."

Calhoun snorted skeptically. "A guide? Why don't I just make you ship's cook while I'm at it?"

"Captain," said Si Cwan, taking a step forward. Kebron growled warningly low in his throat, and it sounded like two asteroids crunching together. Si Cwan stopped where he was and wisely took a step back. "You are entering my home. My backyard, as you would call it. Quite simply, it would be the height of stupidity to toss aside any potential resource. The question becomes: Are you a stupid man?"

"Watch your tone," Zak Kebron warned him.

"Now, if you wouldn't mind, Captain, considering my candor . . . how *did* you know that I had smuggled myself aboard in that cargo?"

"Mislabeling, actually. Several bills of lading had been misplaced, and technicians were using tricorders to run quick scans on cargo contents. Saved us having to go through them box by box."

"Clerical error. I see."

"I'll be discussing this with my senior officers," Calhoun told Si Cwan. "You will remain here until the decision is made. Understood?"

"Your sentiments seem clear enough. And Captain . . ."

"Yes?"

"Thank you for your consideration. And thank you, Commander," he said to Shelby with a small smile, "for not permitting me to be broken in half."

"Don't mention it," she told him generously.

Zak Kebron stepped out and reactivated the force-field as Shelby and Calhoun headed down the hall. As soon as they were out of earshot, Shelby told him with confidence, "I'm feeling a bit better."

"Are you."

"Yes. Because although our three years together

gives us a degree of emotional baggage, it also means we can be in synch on some things without a lot of preplanning."

"Such as?"

"Well, just before. When we slipped into that 'tough cop, nice cop' routine."

He stopped and stared at her. *"What* are you talking about?"

"'Cop.' Old Earth slang for a law-enforcement official. When they would question someone, two of the law officials would work in tandem, one being threatening, the other conciliatory, in order to manipulate the person being questioned. Tough cop, nice cop."

"Never heard of it." He started to walk away but she put a hand on his upper arm, stopping him.

For a moment she felt the hardness of his muscle and thought, *Well, he's certainly kept working out.* Out loud, though, she said, "You weren't *really* going to have Kebron break him in half."

Calhoun smiled in a manner so mysterious that even the Mona Lisa would have been hard-pressed to find fault with it, and then he walked away, leaving Shelby shaking her head before heading up to the bridge.

"So he 'covered' for me," Soleta said. It was not a question; it was as if she knew ahead of time.

"You don't sound surprised," Calhoun said.

"I try never to sound surprised. In this instance, though . . . I simply am not."

Soleta, Calhoun, and Shelby were in the captain's

ready room. Calhoun was leaning slightly back, his feet up on his desk. "Why not?" asked Shelby.

"His desire was to get aboard the vessel. He accomplished that. There would have been no advantage at all in informing you of my duplicity. *Alleged* duplicity," she amended.

Shelby looked to Calhoun for an answer that she already knew. "So Soleta came to you with her dilemma, and you approved her 'sneaking' him aboard."

"That's correct. Problem with that?"

"Several, the most prominent being your not telling me beforehand. But putting that aside—I am going to make the educated guess that you intend to let him remain aboard."

"It is a logical assumption," Soleta agreed. Although the remark was addressed to Shelby, her gaze remained fixed on Calhoun. "After all, I warned the captain before we loaded the hidden Si Cwan onto the ship. We could just as easily have left him behind." Calhoun inclined his head slightly to indicate his concurrence with her astute observation.

"All right, then," Shelby said readily. "That being the case, why in the world did you go through all the subterfuge? Why did you act surprised? Why did you go through this entire song and dance?"

Calhoun draped his hands behind his head and leaned back in his chair. "I know Si Cwan's type, Commander. Hell, I've *fought* his type. The first and foremost consideration is ego. The second is pride. He's part of a ruling class, and is accustomed to doing things his way, even if that way is tremendously involved. In a way, Commander, you should be able to appreciate his point of view."

"How so?"

"Because he cared about two things: the chain of command, and settling a matter of honor. He did not wish to undercut superior officers, but he felt that Soleta owed him a debt since he helped save her life back on Thallon years ago. And you, Lieutenant, were correct to come to me with this situation."

"I saw no logical alternative. Basically, he was correct . . . I did owe him a debt of gratitude. By the same token, I owe my allegiance to Starfleet." She paused a moment. "Do you think that he knew I'd go to you and 'arrange' for him to sneak on, knowing all the time that it would be a setup?"

"Lieutenant, you can lose your mind if you try to think these things through too much."

"So what do we do, Captain? Do we let him stay?" asked Shelby.

"Of course we let him stay. As Soleta pointed out, I wouldn't have allowed him on, subterfuge or no, if I didn't intend to let him stay put."

"But why?"

He leaned back in his chair. "Because I've heard good things about him through the grapevine. Despite his position as part of the ruling family, he was—is—a man of compassion. One doesn't encounter many of those, and if nothing else, I'm intrigued enough to want to study him close up. I figure that he may give us some degree of insight into the Thallonian mind-set, if nothing else. The bottom line is, he may be an officious, arrogant ass, but he's a well-regarded officious, arrogant ass. So I reasoned that he might as well be *our* officious, arrogant ass."

"We can't have too many, I suppose," replied Shelby.

He opened his mouth to continue his train of thought, but the train was abruptly derailed as Shelby's comment sunk in. "Meaning?"

"Nothing, sir," deadpanned Shelby. "Simply an observation."

"Mm-hmm." He didn't appear convinced. But he allowed it to pass, and turned to Soleta. "All right, Lieutenant. Seeing as how he's your pal and all . . ."

"Pal?" She turned the odd word over in her mouth.

". . . go spring him from the brig, on my authority. Coordinate with Lefler and get him set up in quarters."

"Diplomatic?"

"Like hell. Crew quarters will suffice. We wouldn't want him to get any more of a swelled head than he's already got. Inform him, however, that he is on parole. We'll be keeping an eye on him. If he tries anything the least bit out of kilter, he's going to wind up as smear marks on Zak Kebron's boots. That will be all, Lieutenant. Oh, and Lieutenant," he added as an afterthought, "schedule some time for department heads to meet. I want a scientific overview of Thallon. I intend to make that our first stop."

"Straight to the homeworld?" Soleta raised an eyebrow. "Do you expect trouble with achieving that rather incendiary destination?"

"Expect it? No. Anticipate it? Always."

She nodded, an ever-so-brief smile playing on her lips and then quickly hidden by long practice, as she exited the ready room. When she was gone, Shelby folded her arms and half-sat on the edge of Calhoun's desk. "May I ask how you think Admiral Jellico will react to this development? He was the one who originally forbade Si Cwan from joining the mission."

"I imagine that he will be quite angry."

"And out of a sense of morbid curiosity, was this anticipated reaction part of your motivation in allowing Si Cwan to remain?"

"A part? Yes. A major part? No. The good admiral caused me grief in the past, and I certainly don't mind tossing some aggravation his way. But if I didn't think Si Cwan could be useful on this voyage, I wouldn't have allowed him on the ship just to annoy Jellico. That's simply . . ." He paused and then, for lack of a better word, he said, ". . . a bonus."

Si Cwan surveyed his quarters with a critical eye. Soleta and Zak Kebron stood just inside the doorway. After what seemed an infinity of consideration, Si Cwan turned to them and said, "I assume your captain did not give me diplomatic quarters because he did not wish to aggrandize my sense of self-importance."

"He didn't phrase it quite that way, but that is essentially correct."

Si Cwan nodded a moment, and then he looked at Kebron. "I would like a moment's privacy with Soleta." Kebron's gaze flickered between the two of them with suspicion. "Kebron, you'll have to leave me on my own sooner or later," Si Cwan reminded him. "Unless you were planning to make guarding me your life's work."

"It's my life," Kebron replied.

"We'll be fine, Zak," said Soleta, placing a reassuring hand on Kebron's arm. Kebron leaned slightly forward and Si Cwan realized that that was how Kebron nodded, since his neck wasn't the most maneuverable. The Brikar stepped back out of the room and the door closed.

"You and Kebron seem to share a certain familiarity with one another."

"We studied together at Starfleet Academy."

"And study was all you did?"

"No. We also saved one another's lives on occasion. You see the world rather oddly, Si Cwan. May I ask why you wished to speak privately?"

"I," and he cleared his throat. "I wanted to thank you for helping me."

"You're welcome."

"I hope I did not force you to compromise yourself in any way."

"It's a bit late now to be concerned about that," Soleta told him.

"That's valid enough, I suppose. Still I," and for a second time he cleared his throat. "I would like to think that perhaps the two of us could be . . . friends."

"Yes . . . I am sure you would like to think that." And she turned and left him alone in his quarters.

BURGOYNE

VIII.

BURGOYNE 172 PROWLED Engineering in a manner evocative of a cheetah. The *Excalibur* had only been out of drydock for a little over twenty-four hours, and Burgoyne had already established a reputation for perfection that kept hish engineering staff on their collective toes. Burgoyne stopped by the anti-matter regulators and studied the readouts carefully. "Torelli!" s/he called. "Torelli, get your butt down here and bring the rest of you along for the ride!"

Engineer's Mate Torelli seemed to materialize almost by magic at Burgoyne's side.

"Yes, shir," said Torelli.

"I thought I gave you instructions that would improve the energy flow by five percent, and I asked for them to be implemented immediately."

"Yes, shir."

"Did you implement them?"

"Yes, shir."

"Then may I ask why I'm only seeing an improvement of three percent?"

"I don't know, shir."

"Then I suggest you find out." At that moment, Burgoyne's comm badge beeped. S/he tapped it and said, "Chief Engineer Burgoyne here."

"Chief, this is Maxwell down in sickbay. Dr. Selar would like a word with you."

"Can it wait?"

"It's been waiting for a while, shir. She was most emphatic." Maxwell sounded just a touch nervous.

"In other words, we're definitely in the realm of not taking no for an answer, correct?"

"A fair assessment, shir."

Burgoyne sighed. S/he'd been expecting this, really. S/he'd had hish head buried down in Engineering, overseeing every aspect of the refit. Burgoyne would have preferred another two weeks to complete the refit to hish satisfaction, but Starfleet had seemed bound and determined to get them out into space. It was Starfleet's call to make, of course, but Burgoyne couldn't say that s/he was happy about it.

And now the doctor, whom Burgoyne had barely had a chance to take note of in passing, wanted to see hir about some damned thing or other.

"On my way," said Burgoyne, who then glanced up at Torelli and said, "Be sure that's attended to by the time I get back."

"Yes, shir."

"By the way . . . first thing I'd do is make sure that

the problem isn't in the readings rather than in the actual tech. If an object measures a meter long, and the meter stick is wrong, then that doesn't make the object a meter, now, does it."

"No, shir."

"Get on that, then," said Burgoyne. "And don't disappoint me. I don't take well to it. Last person who disappointed me, I ripped their throat out with my teeth."

"You certainly like to joke, Chief," Torelli said.

"That's true, Torelli, I do," Burgoyne agreed. S/he headed for the door and paused there only long enough to say, "Of course, that doesn't mean I was joking just now." And s/he flashed hish sharp canines and walked out.

Soleta and Zak Kebron stepped out onto the bridge to find that all attention was on navigator Mark McHenry.

He was leaning back in his chair, eyes half-closed. He didn't seem to be breathing. Lefler was staring at him, as was Shelby. Calhoun was just emerging from his ready room and he looked to see where everyone else's attention was. He blinked in mild surprise. "Is he dead?" he inquired in a low voice.

"We're trying to determine that," said Lefler.

Shelby looked extremely steamed, but then Calhoun waggled his finger to his senior officers, indicating they should convene in his office. Within moments Robin Lefler found herself alone on the bridge, staring in wonderment at the apparently insensate astronavigator.

Calhoun, for his part, was wondering if he was ever going to get the hell out of his ready room and onto the bridge. Just to be different, he leaned on the armrest of his couch as Shelby said impatiently, "This is insane. We can't have a navigator who falls asleep at his station . . . if that's what he's doing . . ."

"He's not asleep," Soleta told Shelby with authority. "He's just thinking. He's very focused."

"Thinking?" Shelby couldn't believe it. She looked to Calhoun as if she needed verification for what she was hearing. "Captain, it's absurd . . . !"

"I was warned McHenry was somewhat unusual," admitted Calhoun. "I thought he'd fit right in on that basis. But even I'm not sure now . . ."

"Lieutenant Soleta is right," Kebron said, backing her up. "McHenry was like this back in the Academy. Actually, he was even more extreme. It's nothing to be concerned about. As the lieutenant said, McHenry's just thinking."

"About what?" demanded Shelby.

"Anything," said Soleta. "Everything. McHenry devotes exactly as much of his brain power as is required for routine duties. If there's an emergency, he'll devote that much more. And he devotes the rest of his brain to other things. Most humans can only concentrate on one thing at a time. McHenry is multifaceted. What you perceive as aberrant behavior is nothing more than what I would term an . . . eccentricity."

"His eyes are half-closed! We can't have a man at helm who's not alert!"

"He's alert, Commander," Soleta said confidently. "He's one hundred percent alert. If you walked over to him and spoke his name, he'd snap to instantly."

"Responding to his name isn't what concerns me," Shelby replied.

"Nor I," admitted Calhoun. "We need someone at that post who can respond to developing situations on his own, not a man who has to wait for someone to tell him what to do."

"May I suggest a simple test?" asked Soleta. When Calhoun gestured for her to continue, she said, "I can have Lefler reroute guidance through the ops station. Then we'll have her make a change in course. Nothing major. A simple alteration."

"What will that prove?" Shelby asked.

"A great deal, if I am correct," Soleta replied.

"You're not saying that he'll detect, without instruments, a deviation in ship's heading."

"That is precisely what I'm saying, Commander."

"That's impossible," Shelby said flatly. "That is completely impossible."

"Captain," Kebron spoke up, "Commander . . . I fully admit that I had the same initial reactions to McHenry when I met him years ago as you are currently having. I recommend you do as Lieutenant Soleta suggests."

Calhoun shrugged. "Sounds like a plan."

"Captain—?!"

"Calm down, Shelby. Soleta has something to prove. Let's let her try and prove it."

Soleta exited the captain's ready room and went

straight over to Lefler. The others emerged and watched, fascinated in spite of themselves. Soleta bent in close to a puzzled Lefler and whispered in her ear. There was no sign of comprehension on Lefler's face, but she wasn't about to dispute a straightforward instruction. Within moments she had rerouted the navigations systems, and then made a course adjustment that would take the *Excalibur* eighteen degrees off course.

The moment the ship began to move in the new direction, the reaction from McHenry was instantaneous and stunning. He snapped forward, his attention completely focused—not on his instrumentation, but on the starfield in front of him on the screen. He then looked to his instruments, but clearly it was only to confirm that which he already knew. All business, he demanded, "Lieutenant, did you take us off course?"

Shelby was thunderstruck. "I don't believe it," she said. McHenry looked over to her, clearly not sure what Shelby was talking about.

"She changed headings at my direction, Lieutenant McHenry," Soleta informed him.

He switched his focus to Soleta, his eyebrows knit in puzzlement. "Why?"

"Why do you think?"

He considered the question a moment. "Because there was concern that I had zoned out and you decided to prove otherwise?"

"Correct."

"Ah. Okay."

"Without looking at your instruments, Lieutenant," Calhoun said, descending down the ramp to the command chair, "would you mind telling me how far off course we are?"

"I don't know, sir. Ballpark . . . nineteen degrees."

"Eighteen," Robin Lefler acknowledged in wonderment.

"Fairly close ballpark, I'd say," Calhoun said. "Would you agree, Commander?"

Shelby sighed. "Damned close."

"Lieutenant McHenry, bring us back on course."

"Aye, sir."

Shelby sank into her chair. Calhoun sat next to her. "You all right, Commander?"

"Fine," she sighed. "I'm fine. I swear, though, this is like no other ship I've ever served on."

"I'll take that as a compliment," Calhoun said.

"You are, of course, always free to exercise your discretion as commanding officer," Shelby replied, as she wondered what other oddities would surface about the crew during their voyage.

Burgoyne 172 strode into sickbay with an impatient look on hish face. S/he turned to Dr. Maxwell and said, "Well?"

"Well what, Lieutenant Commander?"

"Dr. Selar said she wanted to see me. Here I am. I have things to do, so if the doctor could please tell me what she wants, I might be able to get back to my duties."

Selar emerged from her office and said, "In here, Mister Burgoyne, if it is not too much trouble." She stood there as Burgoyne appeared to be studying her. "Is there a problem, Mister Burgoyne?"

"No. No problem at all," Burgoyne said as s/he entered Selar's office. "You know, I don't think we've actually had a chance to meet."

"You have not attended any of the initial department-head meetings," replied Selar. "That would have been the logical place."

"I had a lot to do to get things ready," Burgoyne said, not sounding particularly apologetic. It seemed to Selar that s/he was looking over the Vulcan doctor in a startlingly appraising manner. "It always comes down to the chief engineer having to pull everything together during the last minute. So . . . what can I do to help you, Doctor?"

"Your most recent medical examination is over two years old. By putting out to space without a more recent exam, we are technically already in breach of Starfleet regulations."

"Can't have that," Burgoyne said agreeably. "Do you wish to conduct it right now? Because I'm free now."

"Dr. Maxwell will attend to the actual examination."

Burgoyne made no effort to hide hish disappointment. "I would prefer you do it. Have the top woman attend to it, and all that."

She glanced at him with eyebrow cocked in mild curiosity. "Do you have an unusual condition which would require my direct attention?"

"Well . . . no . . ."

"Then I assure you, Dr. Maxwell will prove more than sufficient for your needs." She turned and became immediately engrossed in her computer screen, familiarizing herself with other medical profiles. It took her a few moments to realize that Burgoyne was still there, and looking at her with a very strange lopsided grin. "Is there something else, Lieutenant Commander?"

Burgoyne dropped into a chair opposite Selar, giving her the impression that s/he wasn't about to leave anytime soon. "Well, I admit if nothing else I'm disappointed in you, Doctor."

"How so?"

"There aren't very many Hermats in Starfleet, and none at command level aside from me. The Vulcans I know have always had a great inquisitiveness about the galaxy they live in and the people therein. I would be surprised if you, a woman of science, did not share that famed Vulcan drive to satisfy curiosity."

She gave a brief acknowledging nod. "A small amount, I admit. Hermats, as a race, tend to keep to themselves. The tendency toward segregation from the rest of the Federation is well known . . . right down to your tendency to refer to yourselves with a unique set of pronouns to accommodate your dual-sex status. 'Hir' rather than 'him' or 'her' . . . 'hish' for the possessive forms of 'his' or 'hers' . . . 's/he,'" and she punched a bit harder than usual on the separately accented *h,* "rather than 'she' or 'he.'"

"We developed those actually to simplify direct communication with UFP representatives, and also to maintain our uniqueness as a race. Actually, we were originally going to combine 'she,' 'he,' and 'it' in order to cover all possibilities, but the term we developed—'sheeit'—caused Terrans to laugh whenever we would use it, so we surmised that it had some other, inappropriate meaning and discarded it."

"That was probably wise." She paused a moment. "Is there a significant distinction between the Hermat and the J'naii?"

"The J'naii?!" Burgoyne made an annoyed sound. "Those asexual, passionless creatures? No, no. They're neuters, denying all orientation. We celebrate the duality that makes us unique. They are neither. We are both. Fully functioning male and female capabilities." S/he leaned forward and grinned, displaying hish sharpened canines. S/he seemed to be someone who smiled a great deal and enjoyed it while doing so, as s/he repeated, *"Fully* functioning."

"I comprehend the adverb," Selar said evenly. "However, I am quite certain my curiosity about the medical uniqueness of Hermats will be more than satisfied by my scrutiny of Dr. Maxwell's no-doubt detailed examination. For my part, I have a good deal that remains to which I must attend, and a routine exam which could be handled by any first-year resident does not fall into that category. Good day, Lieutenant Commander."

Burgoyne's smile widened as s/he got up from the chair. Hish voice was light and musical as s/he said, "There's one thing you should know about me, Doctor."

"Only one thing. Very well." Selar looked up with poorly veiled disinterest.

"I can sense when I'm going to get on well with someone," Burgoyne informed her. "There's something about the two of us . . . some chemistry . . .

that I can't quite discern yet. But it's there all the same."

Folding her fingers, Selar said, "I am unclear as to your implication, Lieutenant Commander."

"Would you like me to clarify it?"

She considered for a moment and then said, "No. Actually, upon reflection, I prefer the vagueness. Good day, Lieutenant Commander."

"But—"

"I said . . . good day."

S/he stabbed a finger at Selar and said, "You're a challenge. I like a challenge."

"If that is what you desire, I understand surviving in a vacuum can be most challenging. If you wish, I can arrange to have you try that right now, and we can combine your examination with an autopsy."

Burgoyne laughed that delighted musical laugh and coquettishly ran hish fingers through hish close-cut blond hair. "Why, Dr. Selar . . . was that a threat?"

"Not at all. Merely that famed Vulcan drive to satisfy curiosity."

And with one final, lilting laugh and a toss of hish head, Burgoyne sashayed out of Selar's office, leaving the Vulcan doctor shaking her head and wondering two things:

What could she have possibly said or done that would have led Burgoyne 172 to think that there was a fragment of interest on Selar's part in hir?

And why was it that, as Burgoyne walked, Selar found herself watching the sway of hish hips?

IX.

CALHOUN LOOKED AROUND the conference lounge and nodded in approval. "Commander Shelby . . . Lieutenants Soleta and McHenry . . . Ambassador Si Cwan . . . Lieutenant Kebron . . . thank you all for coming . . ." He paused. "Although frankly, Mr. Kebron, I'm not entirely sure if your presence is required here."

"This will be the ambassador's first meeting with you, Captain, without a protective barrier between you. I feel it best if I be here to supervise."

"Yes, your Mr. Kebron has become somewhat attached to me as of late," Si Cwan said dryly. "I would have liked to think that he is fascinated by my sterling company. In point of fact, he's likely concerned I'll disassemble the ship bolt by bolt while his back is turned."

"Merely exercising reasonable caution in the presence of a party with questionable security clearance," Kebron replied.

Calhoun had the distinct feeling that Kebron's comment was a veiled jab at Calhoun himself. Kebron had made no secret that he was unhappy over Si Cwan's unorthodox (to say the least) means of joining the crew, even in a limited, semiofficial capacity. Nor was he any happier over Calhoun's condoning it. However, the Brikar was not one to question his captain's decisions, and so he endeavored to keep his doubts and criticisms to himself. He wasn't terribly good at it—his body language was generally a dead giveaway, as was his tendency to grind his large fingers into his palm with a scrape like rock on rock whenever he was particularly annoyed about something.

"Very wise, Mr. Kebron," Calhoun said diplomatically.

"I do appreciate the title of 'Ambassador,' Captain," Si Cwan commented. "Will quarters appropriate to the title likewise be issued me?"

Calhoun leaned forward and, keeping that same polite, diplomatic tone, said, "That cook job is still open."

"Understood," Si Cwan said in a neutral tone.

With a satisfied nod, Calhoun turned his attention to Soleta. "All right, science officer. You and Mr. McHenry have been working tandem, I understand?"

"Yes, sir. I've been talking extensively with Si Cwan to supplement my own knowledge of Thallon . . ."

"And I've always been something of a history buff," McHenry put in. "So I volunteered to help out with some separate research."

"Good to see, Mr. McHenry," Shelby said approvingly. She wasn't simply being flattering, either. McHenry's clear focus and relatively normal behavior ever since the earlier incident had mollified her concerns to some degree. "What have we got?"

Soleta and McHenry exchanged glances, and she nodded to him that he should begin. He ran his fingers through his shock of red hair, a slight nervous habit, and then said, "Thallon has achieved a nearly mythic status, from everything that I've been able to determine. For starters, the Thallonians were not native to the region. Thallon gained its start as a populated world in much the same way that Australia began."

"You mean criminals?" Kebron said. He made no effort to hide his distaste. In truth, he couldn't have hidden it even if he'd been so inclined.

"That's right. There was another race, a sort of *Uber* race, which had a variety of names as they were known by assorted worlds which were under their influence. The name they had for themselves is lost to history. They were a star-spanning empire who were, if we judge by their conduct, big believers in conquest but also tended to preserve life rather than destroy it, even if it was of no use to them. They used the planet we now call Thallon as a sort of dumping ground for criminals, unsavory types, political exiles . . . assorted refuse from throughout their system."

"It was, at the time, a small, cold, and not

especially fertile world," Soleta added. "It may very well be that they did not expect any of the residents there to survive. Mr. McHenry has chosen to give a somewhat humanitarian spin to this *Uber* race's motivations, but for all we know, they simply regarded Thallon as an experiment in endurance. They may have wanted to see how long individuals could survive there before expiring from the harsh conditions."

"So they simply kept dumping criminals onto this inhospitable world?" asked Shelby.

Soleta shook her head. "Not precisely. From archaeological records and the myths put forward by Si Cwan's people, the first of the Thallonians arrived in what we would call space arks. They were given provisions enough to last them a few months, plus materials to seed the ground and try to make a life for themselves there."

"Seed unfertile ground," Calhoun mused. "The parent race was all heart."

"Yeah, but apparently they weren't all-knowing." McHenry picked up the story. "The exiles were sent to a planet that had been described to them as inhospitable. But that's not what they discovered when they arrived there. The climate was fairly temperate, the world almost paradisiacal."

"Could they have arrived at the wrong planet?" asked Shelby.

"A logical conclusion," Soleta replied. "However, the coordinates for the intended homeworld of the criminals had been preset and locked into the ark's guidance systems. After all, the race didn't want to have their exiles taking control of the ship and heading off to whatever destination they chose. There do remain several possibilities. One is that the planet underwent some sort of atmospheric change. A shift in its axis, for example, causing alterations in the climate."

"Wouldn't that have changed the orbit and made the locating coordinates incorrect, though?" Shelby said.

"Yes," admitted Soleta. "Another possibility is that the present coordinates were simply wrong and they did not arrive at the intended world. Or perhaps someone within their race simply took pity on them and secretly made the change. It is frustrating to admit, but we simply do not know to a scientific certainty."

"What we do know," McHenry stepped in, "is that Thallon itself was an almost limitless supply of pure energy."

"Pure energy? I don't follow," Kebron said.

"Think of it as an entire world made of dilithium crystals," explained Soleta. "Not that it was dilithium per se, but that's the closest comparison. The ground is an energy-rich mineral unique to the world, all-purpose and versatile beyond anything that has ever been discovered elsewhere. The nutrients in it are such that anything planted in it grows. *Anything.* Pieces of the planet, when refined, were used to harness great tools of peace and growth . . ."

"And then, eventually, great tools of war," McHenry said.

The tenor of the meeting seemed to change

slightly, and when the mention of war came up, eyes seemed to shift to Si Cwan. He shrugged, almost as if indifferent. "It was before my time," he reminded them.

"With Thallon as their power base, they were able to launch conquest of neighboring worlds," McHenry said. "And then, once they had those worlds consolidated under their rule, they spread their influence and power to other nearby systems. In essence, they imitated the race which had deposited them there in the first place."

"What about this race you mentioned," asked Calhoun. "Was there a conflict with them? Did they ever return to Thallon and discover what they had wrought? Or did the Thallonians ever go looking for them?"

"No to the first, yes to the second," McHenry replied. "But they never found them. It's one of the great mysteries of Thallonian history."

"And great frustrations," Si Cwan put in.

"Understandable," Kebron rumbled. "Your ancestors wished to pay them back for the initial indignity of being dumped like refuse on another world."

"You see, Lieutenant Kebron," Si Cwan said with mild amusement, "you understand the Thallonians all too well. Perhaps we shall be fast friends, you and I."

Kebron simply stared at him from the depths of his dark, hardened skin.

"The Thallonian homeworld has always been the source of the Thallonian strength, both physical and spiritual," said Soleta. "The events of the last weeks, including the collapse of their empire, may have been presaged by the change in the planet's own makeup. In recent decades, the planet seemed to lose much of its energy richness."

"Why?" asked Calhoun.

"Since the Thallonians were never able to fully explain how their world acquired its properties in the first place, there's understandably confusion as to why it would be deserting them now," said Soleta. "Still, the Thallonians might have been able to withstand those difficulties, if there had not been problems with various worlds within the Thallonian Empire."

"It was the Danteri," Si Cwan said darkly.

Calhoun seemed to stiffen upon the mention of the name. "You claimed that at the *Enterprise* meeting, I understand. Do you have any basis for that?"

"The Danteri have always hungered to make inroads into our empire. They've made no secret of that, nor of their boastfulness. I believe that they instigated rebellion through carefully selected agents. If not for them, we could have—"

"Could have retained your power?"

"Perhaps, Captain. Perhaps."

"By the same token, isn't it possible," Calhoun said, leaning forward, fingers interlaced, "that the Danteri simply serve as a convenient excuse for the deficiencies in your own rule. That it was as a result of ineptitude among the rulers of the Thallonian Empire that the entire thing fell apart. That, in short . . . it was your own damned fault?"

There was dead silence in the room for a moment, and then, imperturbably, Si Cwan said once again,

"Perhaps, Captain. Perhaps. We all have our limitations . . . and we all have beliefs which get us through the day. In that, I assume we are no different."

"Perhaps, Si Cwan. Perhaps," said Calhoun with a small smile.

Then Calhoun's comm unit beeped at him. He tapped it. "Calhoun here."

"Captain, this is Lefler. We're picking up a distress signal from a transport called the *Cambon*."

"Pipe it down here, Lieutenant."

There was a momentary pause, and then it came through the speaker. "This is the *Cambon*," came a rough, hard-edged and angry voice, "Hufmin, Captain. We've sustained major damage in passing through the Lemax system. Engines out, life-support damaged. We have nearly four dozen passengers aboard—civilians, women and children—we need help." His voice seemed to choke on the word, as if it were an obscenity to them. "Repeating, to anyone who can hear . . . this is . . ." And then the signal ceased.

"Lefler, can we get them back?"

"We never had them, sir. We picked it up on an all-band frequency. He threw a note in a bottle and hoped someone would pick it up."

"Have we got a fix on their location?"

"I can track it back and get an approximate. If their engines are out, I can't pinpoint it precisely. On the other hand, they wouldn't have gone too far with no engine power."

"Our orders are to head straight for Thallon," Shelby pointed out.

Calhoun glanced at her. "Are you going to suggest that we ignore a ship in distress, Commander?"

There was only the briefest of pauses, and then Shelby replied, "Not for an instant, Captain. We're here for humanitarian efforts. It would be nothing short of barbaric to then ignore the first opportunity to deploy those efforts."

"Well said. McHenry, get up to the bridge and work with Lefler to find that ship. Get us there at fastest possible speed. Shelby—"

But she was already nodding, one step ahead of him as she tapped her comm unit. "Shelby to engine room."

"Engine room. Burgoyne here."

"Burgy, we're going to be firing up to maximum warp. You have everything ready to go?"

"For you, Commander? Anything. We're fully up to spec. Even I'm satisfied with it."

"If it meets your standards, Burgy, then it must measure up. Shelby out."

McHenry was already on his way, and Calhoun was half-standing. "If there's nothing else . . ."

But Si Cwan was shaking his head, as if discouraged about something. The gesture caught Calhoun's attention, and he said, "Si Cwan?"

"The Lemax system. I know the area. He must have tried to run the Gauntlet. It shouldn't have been a problem." He sighed.

"The Gauntlet?"

"It's a shooting gallery. Two planets that used to be at war, until we imposed peace upon them. The Gauntlet was a hazard of the past, except apparently the danger has been renewed. Just another example of the breakdown occurring all around us." He shook his head again, and then looked around at the silent faces watching him. And then, without another word, he rose and walked out of the room.

Si Cwan stared at the wall of his quarters. Then he heard the sound of the chime. He ignored it, but it sounded again. "Come," he said with a sigh.

Calhoun entered and just stood there, arms folded. "You left rather abruptly."

"I felt the meeting was over."

"Generally it's good form for the captain to make that judgment."

"I am somewhat out of practice in terms of having others make judgments on my behalf."

Calhoun walked across the room, pacing out the interior much as Si Cwan had earlier. "How do you wish to be viewed aboard this ship, Cwan? As an object of pity?"

"Of course not," Si Cwan said sharply.

"Contempt, then? Confusion, perhaps?" He stopped and turned to face him. "Your title, accorded out of courtesy more than anything else, is 'Ambassador.' Not prince. Not lord. 'Ambassador.' I will hope you find that satisfactory. And by the same token, I hope you understand and acknowledge my authority on this ship. I do not want my decision to allow you to remain with us to be viewed by you as lack of strength on my part."

"No. I don't view it that way at all."

"I'm pleased to hear that."

Si Cwan regarded him thoughtfully for a moment. "May I ask how you got that scar?"

Calhoun touched it reflexively. "This one?"

"It is the most prominent, yes."

"To be blunt . . . I got it while killing someone like you."

"I see. And should I consider that a warning?"

"I don't have to kill anymore . . . I hope," he added as an afterthought.

They sat in silence for a moment, and then Si Cwan said, "It is important to me that you understand my situation, Captain. We oversaw an empire, yes. In many ways, in your terms, we might have been considered tyrannical. But it was my life, Captain. It was my life, and the life of those around me who worked to maintain it and help it prosper. Whether you agree with our methods or not, there was peace. There was *peace,*" and he slapped his legs and rose. He turned his back to Calhoun and leaned against the wall, palms spread wide. "Peace built by my ancestors, maintained by my generation. We had a birthright given to us, an obligation . . . and we failed. And now I'm seeing the work of my ancestors, and of my family, dismantled. In a hundred years . . . in ten years, for all I know . . . it will be as if everything we accomplished, for good or ill, will be washed away. Gone. As traceable as a tower of sand on the edge of a beach, consumed by the rising tide. What we did will have made no difference. It was all for nothing. Every difficult decision, every hard choice, ultimately amounted to nothing whatsoever. We have no legacy for our future generations. Indeed, we'll probably have no future generations. I have no royal consort with whom I can perpetuate our line. No royal lineage to pass on."

"And you're hoping to use this vessel to rebuild your power base. Aren't you."

Si Cwan turned and stared at him. "Is that what you think?"

"It's crossed my mind."

"I admit it crossed mine as well. But I give you my word, Captain, that I will do nothing to endanger this ship's mission, nor any of its personnel. My ultimate goal is the same as yours: to serve as needed."

Slowly Calhoun nodded, apparently satisfied. "All right. I can accept that . . . for now."

"Captain . . . ?"

"Yes."

Si Cwan smiled thinly. "You were aware the entire time, weren't you. Aware that I had stowed away on your vessel."

For a moment Calhoun considered lying, a course that he would not hesitate to indulge in if he felt that it would serve his purposes. But his instinct told him that candor was the way to go in this matter. "Yes."

"Good."

"Good?"

"Yes. It is something of a relief, really. The notion that I was aboard a ship where the commanding officer had so little awareness of what was happening around him . . . it was unsettling to me."

"I'm relieved that I was able to put your mind at ease. And Si Cwan . . ."

"Yes?"

"Believe it or not . . . I can sympathize. I've had my own moments where I felt that my life had been wasted."

"And may I ask how you dealt with such times of despair?"

And Mackenzie Calhoun laughed softly and said, "I took command of a starship." But then he held up a warning finger. "Don't get any ideas from that."

"I shall try not to, Captain. I shall try very hard."

X.

HUFMIN STARED OUT at the stars and, focusing on one at a time, uttered a profanity for every one he picked out.

Cramped in the helm pit of the *Cambon*, he still couldn't believe that he had gotten himself into this fix. He scratched at his grizzled chin and dwelt for the umpteenth time on the old Earth saying that no good deed goes unpunished.

He glanced at his instrumentation once more, his lungs feeling heavier and heavier. He knew that the last thing you were supposed to do upon receiving a head injury was let yourself fall asleep. And so he had kept himself awake through walking around in the cramped quarters, through stimulants, recitation, biting himself—anything and everything he could think of. None of which was going to do him a damned bit of good because, just to make things absolutely perfect, he wasn't going to be able to breathe for all that much longer. The life-support systems were tied into his engines. When they went down, the support systems switched to backup power supply, but that was in the process of running out. Hufmin was positive it was getting tougher to breathe, although he wasn't altogether certain how much of that was genuine and how much was just his imagination running away with him. But if it wasn't happening now, it was going to be happening soon enough as the systems became incapable of cleansing the atmosphere within the craft and everybody within suffocated.

Everybody . . .

Every . . . body . . .

. . . lots of bodies.

Not for the first time, he dwelt on the fact that this was a case where the more was most definitely not the merrier. Every single body on the ship was another person who was taking up space, another person breathing oxygen and taking up air that would be better served to keep him, Hufmin, alive.

What had possessed him? What in God's name had possessed him to take on this useless, unprofitable detail? If he'd been a Ferengi he would have been drummed out of . . . well, whatever it was that Ferengi were drummed out of when they made unbelievably bad business decisions. The problem was that this was no longer simply a case of costing him money. Now it was going to cost him his life.

. . . lots of bodies . . .

"Dump 'em," he said, giving voice finally to the thought that had bounced around in his head for the last several hours. It was a perfectly reasonable idea. All he had to do was get rid of the passengers and he could probably survive days, maybe even weeks, instead of the mere hours that his instruments seemed to indicate remained to him.

It wouldn't be easy. There were, after all, forty-seven of them and only one of him. It wasn't likely that they would simply and cheerfully hurl themselves into the void so that he, Hufmin, had a better chance at survival. No, the only way to get rid of them would be by force. Again, though, he was slightly outnumbered . . . by about forty-seven to one.

He had a couple of disruptors in a hidden compartment under his feet. He could remove those, go into the aft section where all the passengers were situated, and just start firing away. Blow them all to hell and gone and then eject the bodies. But then he pictured himself standing there, shooting, body after body going down, seeing the fear of death in their eyes, hearing the death rattles not once, not twice, but forty-seven times. Because it was going to have to be all of them. All or nothing, he knew that with absolute certainty. He couldn't pick and choose. All or nothing. But he was no murderer. He'd never killed anyone in his life; the disruptors were just for protection, a last resort, and he'd never fired them. Never had to. Kill them and then blast them into space . . . how could he . . . ?

Then he realized. He didn't have to kill them. Just blast them into space, into the void. Sure, they'd die agonizingly, suffering in space, but it wasn't as if death by disruptor was all that much better.

The *Cambon* was divided into three sections: The helm pit, which was where he was. The midsection, used for equipment storage mostly, and his private quarters as well. And the aft section . . . the largest section, used for cargo . . .

. . . which was where all his passengers were. They were cramped, they were uncomfortable, but they were alive.

Hufmin's eyes scanned his equipment board. And there, just as he knew it would be, was the control for the aft loading doors. There were controls in back as well, but they were redundant and—if necessary—could be overridden from the helm pit. The helm pit, which was, for that matter, self-contained and secured, a heavy door sealing it off from the rest of the vessel.

All he had to do was blow the loading-bay doors. The passengers back there probably wouldn't even have time to realize that their lives were ended before they were sucked out into the vacuum of space. Granted he'd lose some air as well. With power so low, the onboard systems would never be able to replenish what he lost to the vacuum. On the other hand, he'd have the remaining air in the helm pit and in the midsection. Not a lot, but at least it would be all his. All his.

. . . lots of bodies . . .

The bay-door switch beckoned to him and he reached over and tapped it, determined to do what had to be done for survival before he thought better of it. Immediately a yellow caution light came on, and the operations computer came on in its flat, monotone masculine voice. "Warning. This vessel is not within a planetary atmosphere. Opening of loading-bay doors will cause loss of air in aft section and loss of any objects not properly secured. Do you wish to continue with procedure? Signify by saying, 'Continue with procedure.'"

"Con—" The words caught in his throat.

. . . lots of bodies . . .

"Con . . . contin—"

There was a rapping at the door behind him. It reverberated through the helm pit, like a summons from hell. *"What is it?!"* he shouted at the unseen intruder.

"Mr. Hufmin?" came a thin, reedy voice. A child's voice, a small girl. One of the soon-to-be corpses.

"Yeah? What?"

"I was . . . I was wondering if anyone heard our call for help."

"I don't know. I wish I did, but I don't. Go back and sit with your parents now, okay?"

"They're dead."

That caught him off-guard for a moment, but then he remembered; one of the kids had lost her parents to some rather aggressive scavengers. She was traveling with an uncle who looked to be around ninety-something. "Oh, right, well . . . go back with your uncle, then."

There was a pause and he thought for a moment that she'd done as he asked. He started to address the computer again when he heard, "Mr. Hufmin?"

"What is it, damn you!"

"I just . . . I wanted to say thank you." When he said nothing in response, she continued, "I know you tried your best, and that I know you'll keep trying, and I . . . I believe in you. Thank you for everything."

He stared at the blinking yellow light. "Why are you saying this? Who told you to say this?" he asked tonelessly.

"The gods. I prayed to them for help, and I was starting to fall asleep while I was praying . . . and I heard them in my head telling me to say thank you. So I . . . I did."

Hufmin's mouth moved, but nothing came out. "That's . . . that's fine. You're, uh . . . you're welcome. Okay? You're welcome."

He listened closely and heard the sound of her feet pattering away. He was all alone once more. Alone to do what had to be done.

"Computer."

"Waiting for instructions," the computer told him. The computer wouldn't care, of course. It simply waited to be told. It was a machine, incapable of making value judgments. Nor was it capable of taking any actions that would insure its own survival. Hufmin, on the other hand, most definitely was.

"Computer . . ."

He thought of the child. He thought of the bodies floating in space. So many bodies. And he would survive, or at least have a better chance, and that was the important thing. "Computer, continue with . . ."

What was one child, more or less? One life, or

forty-seven lives? What did any of it matter? The only important thing was that he lived. Wasn't that true? Wasn't it?

He envisioned them floating past his viewer, their bodies destroyed by the vacuum, their faces etched in the horror of final realization. And he would still be alive . . .

. . . and he might as well be dead.

With the trembling sigh of one who knows he has just completely screwed himself, Hufmin said, "Computer, cancel program."

"Canceling," replied the computer. Naturally, whether he continued the program or not was of no consequence to the computer. As noted, it was just a machine. But Hufmin liked to think he was something more, and reluctantly had to admit that—if that was the case—it bore with it certain responsibilities.

He leaned back in his pilot's seat, looked out at the stars, and said, "Okay, gods. Whisper something to *me* now. Tell me what an idiot I am. Tell me I'm a jerk. Go ahead. Let me have it, square between the eyes."

And the gods answered.

At least, that's what it appeared they were doing, because the darkness of space was shimmering dead ahead, fluctuating ribbons of color undulating in circular formation.

Slowly he sat forward, his mind not entirely taking in what he was witnessing, and then the gods exploded from the shadows.

These gods, however, had chosen a very distinctive and blessed conveyance. They were in a vessel that Hufmin instantly recognized as a Federation starship. It had dropped out of warp space, still moving so quickly that it had been a hundred thousand kilometers away and then, an eyeblink later, it was virtually right on top of him. He'd never seen such a vessel in person before, and he couldn't believe the size of the thing. The ship had course-corrected on a dime, angling upward and slowing so that it passed slowly over him rather than smashing him to pieces. He saw the name of the ship painted on the underside: *U.S.S. Excalibur.* The ship was so vast that it blotted out the light provided by a nearby sun, casting the *Cambon* into shadow, but Hufmin could not have cared less.

Hufmin had never been a religious man. The concept of unseen, unknowable deities had been of no interest to him at all in his rather pragmatic life. And as he began to deliriously cheer, and wave his hands as if they could see him, he decided that he did indeed believe in gods after all. Not the unknowable ones, though. His gods were whoever those wonderful individuals were who loomed above him. They had come from wherever it was gods came from, and had arrived in this desperate environment currently inhabited by one Captain Hufmin and his cargo of forty-seven frightened souls.

Thereby answering, finally, a very old question, namely:

What does God need with a starship?

And the answer, of course, was one of the oldest answers in the known universe:

To get to the other side.

XI.

ROBIN LEFLER LOOKED UP from Ops and said, "Captain, everyone from the vessel has been beamed aboard: the ship's commander and forty-seven passengers."

Shelby whistled in amazement as Calhoun said, clearly surprised, "Forty-seven? His ship's not tiny, but it's not *that* big. He must have had people plastered to the ceiling. Shelby, arrange to have the passengers brought, in shifts, to sickbay, so Dr. Selar can check them over. Make sure they're not suffering from exposure, dehydration, et cetera."

"Shall we take his ship in tow, sir?" asked Kebron.

"And to where do you suggest we tow it, Mr. Kebron?" asked Calhoun reasonably. "It's not as if we've got a convenient starbase nearby. Bridge to Engineering."

"Engineering, Burgoyne here," came the quick response over the intercom.

"Chief, we have a transport ship to port with an engine that needs your magic touch."

"My wand is at the ready, sir."

"How many times have I heard *that* line," murmured Robin Lefler . . . just a bit louder than she had intended. The comment drew a quick chuckle from McHenry, and a disapproving glance from Shelby . . . who, in point of fact, thought it was funny but felt that it behooved her to keep a straight face.

"Get a team together, beam over, and give me an estimate on repair time."

"Aye, sir."

He turned to Shelby and said briskly, "Commander, talk to the pilot. Find out precisely what happened, what he saw. I want to know what we're dealing with. Also, see if you can find Si Cwan. He's supposed to be our ambassador. Let's see how his people react to him. If they throw things at him or run screaming, that will be a tip off that he might not be as useful as we'd hoped. Damn, we should have given him a comm badge to facilitate—"

"Bridge to Si Cwan," Shelby said promptly.

"Yes," came Si Cwan's voice.

"Meet me in sickbay, please. We have some refugees there whom we'd like you to speak with."

"On my way."

Shelby turned to Calhoun. "I took the liberty of issuing him a comm badge. He's not Starfleet, of course, but it seemed the simplest way to reach him."

"Good thinking, Commander."

She smiled. "I have my moments," and headed to the turbolift.

The moment she was gone, though, Kebron stepped over to Calhoun and said, "Captain, shall I go as well?"

"You, Kebron? Why?"

"To keep an eye on Cwan."

"What do you think he's going to do?"

"I don't know," Kebron said darkly. He seemed to want to say something more, but he kept his mouth tightly closed.

"Lieutenant, if you've got something on your mind, out with it."

"Very well. I feel that you have made a vast mistake allowing Si Cwan aboard this vessel. He could jeopardize our mission."

"If I believed he could, I would never have allowed him to remain."

"I'm aware of that, sir. Nevertheless, I feel it was an error."

"I generally have a good instinct about people, Lieutenant. I've learned to trust it; it's saved my life any number of times. If you wish to disagree with me, that is your prerogative."

"Then I'm afraid that's how it's going to remain, Captain, until such time as I'm convinced otherwise."

"And when do you think that will be?"

Zak Kebron considered the question. "In Earth years, or in Brikar years?"

"Earth years."

"In Earth years?" He paused only a moment, and then responded, "Never."

Shelby entered sickbay and looked around at the haggard faces of the patients in the medlab. Immediately her heart went out to them. They were a mixture of races, with such variations of skin colors between them that they looked like a rainbow. But there was unity in the fact that they were clearly frightened, dispossessed, with no clear idea of what lay ahead for them. Dr. Selar was going about her duties with efficiency and speed. Shelby noticed that Selar and her people already seemed to be working smoothly and in unison. She felt some relief at that; Calhoun had mentioned that there'd been some difficulty between Selar and one of her doctors, but Shelby wouldn't have known from watching them in action.

"I'm looking for the commander of the vessel," she said to the room at large.

One of the scruffier individuals stepped forward. "That would be me." He stuck out a hand. "Name's Hufmin."

"Commander Shelby, second-in-command."

"You people saved our butts."

"That's what we're here for," she told him, even as she thought, *Did I just* say *that? I sound like something out of the Starfleet Cliché Handbook.*

And then Shelby saw the attitude of the people in sickbay change instantly, as if electrified. A number who were on diagnostic tables immediately jumped off. One even pushed Dr. Selar aside so he could scramble to his feet. They were all looking past

Shelby's shoulder. She turned to see that, standing behind her, was Si Cwan.

There was dead silence for what seemed an infinity to her, and then a young woman, who appeared to be in her early twenties by Earth standards, seemed to fly across the room. She threw her arms around Si Cwan so tightly that it looked as if she'd snap him like a twig, even though she came up barely to his chest.

"You're alive, thank the gods, you're alive," she whispered.

And now the others followed suit. Most of them did not possess the total lack of inhibition of the first woman. They approached him tentatively, reverently, with varying forms of intimidation or respect. Si Cwan, for his part, stroked the young woman's thick blue hair as gently as a father cradling his newborn child. He looked to the others, stretching out his free hand as if summoning them. They seemed to draw strength from his mere presence, many of them genuflecting, a few had their heads bowed.

"Please. Please, that's not necessary," said Si Cwan. "Please . . . get up. Don't bow. Don't . . . please don't," and he gestured for them to rise. "Sometimes I feel that such ceremonies helped create the divide between us that led to . . . to our present state. Up . . . yes, you in the back, up."

They followed his instructions out of long habit. "This ship is bringing you back to power, Lord Cwan?" asked one of the men. "They'll use their weapons on your behalf?"

Shelby began to state that that was uncategorically

not the case, but with a voice filled with surprising gentleness, Si Cwan said, "This is a mission of peace, my friends. I am merely here to lend help wherever I can." And then he glanced briefly at Shelby as if to say, *A satisfactory answer?* She nodded in silent affirmation.

Then Shelby turned back to the refugees and said, "What were you all fleeing from?"

A dozen different answers poured out, all at the same time. The specifics varied from one individual or one group to the next, but there were common themes to all. Governments in disarray, marauders from an assortment of races, wars breaking out all over for reasons ranging from newly disputed boundaries to attempted genocide. A world of order sliding into a world of chaos.

"We just want to be safe," said the young woman who had so precipitously hugged Si Cwan. "Is that too much to ask?"

"Unfortunately," sighed Si Cwan, "sometimes the answer to that is yes."

"The rest of the royal family . . . are they . . . ?"

He nodded and there were a few choked sobs . . . and also, Shelby noted, a few sighs of relief.

"What's going to happen to us now?" asked one of them.

"First, we're going to repair Captain Hufmin's vessel. We have a team there right now," Shelby told them. At this, Hufmin moaned softly and shook his head, which piqued Shelby's curiosity. "Problem, Captain?"

"Well, don't think I'm not grateful for the rescue

and repair. I am. More than you can believe. But I have to ask . . . how much is the repair job going to cost? Because I'm not making the kind of money off this job that you'd probably think I am—"

"Captain Hufmin," Shelby began.

"—and you've got your experts who, I'm sure, are the best that money can buy, but my credit level is so low that unless we set up some sort of payment schedule . . ."

"Captain, there's no charge," Shelby interrupted him.

This brought him up short. "No charge?"

"None."

"Well then . . . what do you get out of this?"

"We get nothing more from it than the awareness that we're fulfilling the mandates of Starfleet. That, and simply the knowledge of a job well done," Shelby told him, and this time she thought, *Dammit, I know I've mostly specialized in fighting the Borg, and have far more strategic bridge experience than I do with one-to-one diplomacy, but I have got to drop the homilies before someone beats me to death with a baseball bat.*

"And then what?" asked another of the refugees.

"Then we'll make sure that you get where you're going. Where are you going, by the way?"

"Intended destination is Sigma Tau Ceti," Hufmin told her. "Not the greatest planet on the rim, but it's within range considering what they were able to pay. Although if you've got other suggestions, I'm sure they'd be happy to discuss it. . . ."

At that moment, Si Cwan's comm badge beeped.

He seemed slightly startled by it since he was, naturally, unused to wearing it. He tapped it tentatively and said, "Yes?"

"Si Cwan, this is Soleta," came the Vulcan's voice. "We've received a communiqué I think you should be aware of."

"What is it?"

"It's another vessel. They not only sent out a distress call, but they included a passenger roster. If I'm recalling correctly, didn't you say your sister's name was Kallinda?"

For a moment Si Cwan felt as if his heart had stopped. "Yes. Yes, I did."

"Well, her name's on it."

"I'm on my way," he said without hesitation. He paused and said to the refugees, "Trust these people. They will take care of you," and then he was out the door, his long legs carrying him so rapidly that Shelby felt as if he'd vanished between eyeblinks.

Hufmin took a step forward and, clearing his throat, said, "Uhm, Commander . . . as long as your people are over there . . . you know, the phase converter's never worked really up to what I'd like. Also I could use a replacement of the dilithium charger, and a full cleaning of the—"

"Hufmin . . ."

"Yes, Commander Shelby?"

She smiled wanly. "Don't push it, okay?"

Inside the midship area of the *Cambon*. Burgoyne shook hish head in annoyance as s/he looked over the damage report. "Interior and exterior damage to the impulse rods, as well as the primary warp stabilizer. And look at the age of some of these parts; I hope we can match it. To say nothing of the fact that we'll have to do EVA repairs." S/he sighed. "This'll take forever."

"Can we bring this ship into the shuttlebay and work on it there?" asked Yates.

Burgoyne shook hish head. "Too big. If we were in a Galaxy-class ship, yes, it'd fit. But in the Ambassador-class size? Not near enough room. Although I suppose if we could bring it close enough in to the *Excalibur,* we could raise shields and encompass it within the shield sphere. Then all we'd need is some floaters to move around it, rather than have to put up with clunky EVA suits. You'd think after four centuries of a space program, we'd have come up with better EVA suits than what we've got." Burgoyne tapped hish comm badge. "Burgoyne to bridge."

"Bridge, Kebron here."

"Zak? Tell the captain we're talking at least a nine-hour repair job here."

"Nine hours?" Kebron sounded skeptical. "You could disassemble the *Excalibur*'s engines and put them back together in nine hours."

"If you think you can do better, Kebron, you're welcome to try. Burgoyne out."

Si Cwan studied the passenger roster with a rapidly growing sense of urgency. "What's the ship's name again?" he asked.

"The *Kayven Ryin,*" Soleta said, coming around from the science station. Si Cwan was at the tactical station, looking over the incoming transmission.

Kebron had at first stood firm, but ultimately backed off a few feet and simply glowered with arms folded. "It's not a Federation ship, but it's in the registry nonetheless. It's a freelance science and exploration vessel."

"Why would a science vessel be carrying any passengers at all, much less Si Cwan's sister?" asked Kebron.

"It makes sense," Si Cwan said with more excitement than Soleta had ever heard in his voice. "You're absolutely right, Kebron, it's not the type of vessel that would be used for transport. Secondly, unless I'm mistaken, it's big."

"Quite big," affirmed Soleta. "Such vessels usually are. Science and exploration vessels generally tend to be prepared for anything. It can easily accommodate a scientific team of up to one hundred people, transporting sufficient life-support equipment to sustain them for—"

"We get the idea, Lieutenant," Calhoun said, rising from his chair and standing on the lower level of the bridge in front of the tactical station. "But according to the manifest, how many passengers in this instance on the *Kayven Ryin?*"

"Only nine, actually."

"I see. How long ago was the message sent?"

"It's still being sent, Captain," Kebron said. "It's on live feed, a steady pulse."

"Try to raise them."

Kebron made that slight bow that passed for a nod and stepped up to tactical. He took a small amount of pleasure in hip-checking Si Cwan out of the way as he sent an autohail back through subspace. While he waited for a response, he watched Si Cwan's reactions carefully. And he could see that Si Cwan was . . .

. . . afraid.

This struck Kebron as unusual, to say the least. He wasn't quite sure what to expect from Si Cwan, but fear hadn't quite been it. Kebron immediately started to become annoyed with himself as he realized he was feeling something for Si Cwan that he didn't want to feel: sympathy. He pushed such annoying thoughts as far away as he could as he reported briskly, "No response."

"How far away are they?"

"Approximately two hours at warp two."

"Captain, we have to go get her," Si Cwan said urgently. "She can't be that close and we don't do anything."

"We're already working on one rescue effort, Ambassador," replied Calhoun. "We finish one before we move on to the next. We can't go running helter-skelter throughout the sector."

"Captain, please," began Si Cwan.

But Calhoun cut him off emphatically. "We have four dozen frightened and shaken-up people on this vessel. I'm not about to start dragging them on side trips."

"A side trip? Captain, there are *lives* involved."

"My decision is final, Ambassador. I'm sorry." He hesitated. "Unless . . ."

"Unless?" demanded Si Cwan with obvious urgency.

Calhoun turned to Lefler and said, "Refresh my memory, Lefler. We have a runabout down in the hangar bay?"

"Aye, sir. The *Marquand.*"

"Can it make warp two?"

"That and a bit more in a pinch."

He nodded and looked back to Si Cwan. "Ambassador . . . we're remaining on station until such time that repairs are completed and we can send our passengers on their way. But if you want to grab a runabout and rendezvous with the *Kayven Ryin,* I'll authorize it."

"That is more than generous, Captain," Si Cwan said. "I'll prepare to leave immediately. . . ."

"Captain!" exclaimed an alarmed Zak Kebron.

"Problem, Mr. Kebron?"

"Sir, as head of security, I must register a formal protest."

"Formal. And me without my dress uniform."

"Sending a non-Starfleet individual out in a runabout . . ." Kebron couldn't find the words.

"On second thought, Mr. Kebron, you're absolutely right."

Zak let out a sigh of relief. "I'm pleased that you—"

"You'll be accompanying him."

"Captain! No, you can't—"

And Calhoun stepped in close to Kebron, and when he spoke his voice was low and angry, and his scar seemed to be standing out against his skin. "I can, and I am. I ask nothing of my crew members but the best they have to offer, and if the best you can offer is insubordination, then I'm going to get a new crew member and you can damn well walk home. Understood?"

"Yes, sir," said Kebron tightly.

"Good." Calhoun stepped back and then his gaze transfixed Si Cwan. "Do you have any problems with Mr. Kebron accompanying you?"

Si Cwan seemed ready to make one response, and clearly thought better of it, and said instead, "None whatsoever."

"Just what I wanted to hear: nothing. Lefler, have the shuttlebay prepare the *Marquand* for departure. Gentlemen . . . have a pleasant flight. And stay in touch. You know how I worry."

XII.

SHELBY STARED INCREDULOUSLY at Calhoun. "You must be out of your mind."

Calhoun looked up from his desk. "I assume you're referring to the errand on which I sent Mr. Kebron and Ambassador Cwan."

"Of course I am! Kebron's made no secret of the fact that he doesn't like Si Cwan. How could you stick the two of them in a runabout together and send them out on a jaunt? We could have broken off from our repairs on the *Cambon*. If we'd left it sitting in space for a few hours while we checked out this other distress signal . . ."

"Nothing would have happened, yes, I know. That wasn't the point."

"Then what was?"

"You've checked out Mr. Kebron's psych profile, I take it?"

"I read over his career highlights, yes. A solid officer . . . no pun intended. Diligent. Thorough."

"Yes, but sometimes he has difficulty . . . oh, what's the old phrase . . . working and playing well with others. Particularly when it comes to races with whom he has little to no familiarity."

"The fact that he's extremely suspicious makes him well suited to being head of Security. You don't want someone who trusts everyone."

"Granted. But you don't want someone who is so distrustful that it impedes his ability to function . . . particularly when it comes to interaction with other crewmen."

"Point taken," said Shelby reluctantly. "Do you have any reason to believe such would be the case with Kebron?"

"There was an incident—a series of incidents, really—during his first year at Starfleet Academy. He apparently wasn't at the Academy for more than five minutes before he got into a brawl with another cadet, who happened to be the first Klingon at the Academy . . ."

"Worf?" asked Shelby in surprise.

"You know him?"

"I've worked with him. He's a . . . unique individual."

"Most individuals are," he observed. "In any event, it appears that Mr. Kebron's tendency to be judgmental and suspicious proved a hindrance, and friction continued between him and Worf. In order to alleviate the problem, the Academy heads forced

Mr. Kebron and Mr. Worf to be roommates. The close proximity prompted an airing out of difficulties and, eventually, a smoothly operating relationship."

"I see. And you decided that pushing Kebron and Si Cwan together for a period of time might smooth out the hostilities in this instance."

"That is my plan, yes. What do you think?"

"Risky and unnecessary. Simply order Kebron to cooperate with Si Cwan and let it go at that."

"I've found that human nature . . . or, for that matter, Brikar or Thallonian nature . . . doesn't generally respond well to . . ."

And then his voice trailed off, and he frowned.

Shelby watched in confusion. "Mac?" she said after a long moment. "What—?"

"We're in trouble," he said.

"What do you mean? What kind of—"

"Captain!" It was Lefler's voice, and there wasn't panic in it, but there was extreme concern. "We've got company!"

Instantly Calhoun was out on the bridge, his attention on the screen. Soleta had moved to the tactical station to cover for the absent Kebron, and she said, "It just dropped out of warp."

The vessel on the screen was approaching them rapidly. It was large and black with silver markings. As a result it almost seemed to be one with the starry background behind it.

"Go to yellow alert. Beam the repair crew off the *Cambon* this instant and then raise shields. Scan it for weaponry," said Calhoun.

"Scanning," she confirmed as the yellow-alert klaxon sounded.

In a low voice, Shelby asked Calhoun, "How the hell did you know?"

"I usually know. It's a knack."

Before she could inquire further, Soleta said, "Scan complete. They possess front- and rear-mounted phase/plasma cannons. Primitive but effective. If we get into a pitched battle, we could be hurt."

"Captain," said Shelby, "They've made no hostile move. With all respect, you can't go into any situation assuming that every vessel you're going to encounter may open fire . . ."

And Lefler suddenly called out, *"Captain, they've opened fire!"*

The silence was thick in the runabout *Marquand*. Kebron was taking great pains not to look in Si Cwan's direction.

"Lieutenant," Si Cwan finally said, "would you mind telling me what your problem is?"

"Problem? I have no problem," said Kebron with exaggerated formality.

"Lieutenant, dissembling ill suits you."

"Are you calling me a liar?" inquired Kebron.

Si Cwan studied him a moment more, and then unstrapped himself from his seat and moved to the aft section of the ship. "All right," he said. "Let's go. Come on."

"What are you talking about?"

"I know what this is about. This is about the fact

that, in your very first assignment as security chief of the *Excalibur,* you were beaten up."

"I was not beaten up."

"Yes, you were. I should know. I was the one who did it."

Kebron tried to get up so quickly that he almost knocked his chair backward . . . which was a formidable feat, considering that it was bolted down. "Knocking me off balance is hardly the same as 'beating me up.'"

"Well, now you'll have the opportunity to prove it." Si Cwan stood in a limber, prepared fashion, his arms poised, his legs slightly bent. "Come on. Take a shot at me. Let's settle this once and for all."

"We're on a mission," Kebron told him angrily. "This is not the time for pointless displays of combat."

"I see. Perhaps you're afraid, then."

"Of you?" Kebron laughed contemptuously. "In a true, honorable fight, you would not stand a chance against me."

"Then let's find out right now."

"No." And Kebron sat back down again.

Si Cwan strode forward. "Why not?"

"Because," he said reasonably, "if your sister is aboard the vessel, do you wish to greet her with your face bruised and battered? I would think she would be frightened to see you in such a state."

Si Cwan laughed curtly. "My being disfigured would not be a factor."

"Your confidence is misplaced."

"As is your hostility. We're on the same side, Kebron."

Keeping his gaze fixed resolutely on the stars streaking past them, Kebron said, "I dislike dictators. I dislike stowaways. And I dislike those who feel they are superior to others. You fall into all three categories. As I'm sure you can surmise, then . . . I dislike you."

For a time, Si Cwan said nothing. And then he drew very close to Kebron and said in a quiet voice that seemed filled with pain, "I've noticed that those who are the most confident that they know another person are the most likely to know the least."

And with that, he sat back down in his seat in the cockpit, and said nothing more for a full hour. Until their sensors told them that the science vessel *Kayven Ryin* was just ahead. Immediately, Kebron began hailing on the subspace radio again, and as he did so, Si Cwan said nothing. Kebron became aware that Si Cwan was holding his breath, and it was an awareness that annoyed him tremendously. For Si Cwan's concern over his sister was going a long way toward "humanizing" Cwan in Kebron's eyes, and it was so much easier to dislike someone when you could find nothing redeemable in their character.

And then a voice came over the radio. Si Cwan jumped so unexpectedly at the sound that he banged his head on the ceiling of the runabout as a voice said, "Incoming vessel . . . this is the *Kayven Ryin.* Are you here to aid us?"

"This is the *Marquand,* dispatched by the *Starship Excalibur,*" Kebron responded. "We are here to provide whatever temporary aid we can, and then report back to the *Excalibur.* In a short time, however, we'll be able to offer you the full services of our main ship."

"Kallinda," Si Cwan was whispering urgently. "Ask them about . . ."

"Your passenger manifest listed a Thallonian named Kallinda," Kebron said. "Is that Kallinda of the deposed royal family of Thallon?"

There was a hesitation on the other end. "We don't generally discuss private matters of our passengers, *Marquand* . . ."

"You have nothing to fear from us, *Kayven Ryin*. We're from Starfleet. We're here for humanitarian aid and," he glanced at the agonizingly eager Si Cwan, "if she is the Kallinda in question . . . I have her brother here."

There was the briefest of pauses. "Si Cwan is there?"

"That is correct, yes."

"Tell him . . . tell him his sister never stops talking about him, and is looking forward to seeing him."

It was all Si Cwan could do to steady himself. Kebron gestured toward the console, silently indicating that if Si Cwan wanted to say something, he could. And Kebron was surprised to see that Cwan clearly could not do so because apparently he didn't trust himself to speak, so choked was he with emotion. "Consider the message passed along. We'll be there within five minutes. . . ."

"We'll be ready for you, *Marquand*. . . ."

. . . and aboard the *Kayven Ryin*, several Thallonians were grouped around the communications board. "We'll be ready for you, *Marquand*," one of them said. Then he snapped off the comm unit, and turned to the most powerfully built of the group, who was sliding a fresh energy clip into the barrel of his plasma blaster. "We will be ready for them . . . won't we, Zoran."

"Oh, yes," said Zoran. "And finally I'll have that reunion with Si Cwan I've so been looking forward to."

And he slammed the clip tightly into place. . . .

To Be Continued

1252.01

STAR TREK
DEEP SPACE NINE™

24" X 36" CUT AWAY POSTER,
7 COLORS WITH 2 METALLIC INKS & A GLOSS AND MATTE VARNISH, PRINTED ON ACID FREE ARCHIVAL QUALITY
65# COVER WEIGHT STOCK INCLUDES OVER 90 TECHNICAL CALLOUTS, AND HISTORY OF THE SPACE STATION.
U.S.S. DEFIANT EXTERIOR, HEAD SHOTS OF MAIN CHARACTERS, INCREDIBLE GRAPHIC OF WORMHOLE.

STAR TREK™
U.S.S. ENTERPRISE™ NCC-1701

24" X 36" CUT AWAY POSTER,
6 COLORS WITH A SPECIAL METALLIC INK & A GLOSS AND MATTE VARNISH, PRINTED ON ACID FREE ARCHIVAL
QUALITY 100# TEXT WEIGHT STOCK INCLUDES OVER 100 TECHNICAL CALLOUTS,
HISTORY OF THE ENTERPRISE CAPTAINS & THE HISTORY OF THE ENTERPRISE SHIPS.

ALSO AVAILABLE:
LIMITED EDITION SIGNED AND NUMBERED BY ARTISTS.
LITHOGRAPHIC PRINTS ON 80# COVER STOCK (DS9 ON 100 # STOCK) WITH OFFICIAL LICENSED CERTIFICATE OF
AUTHENTICITY. QT. AVAILABLE 2,500

AVAILABLE U.S.S. ENTERPRISE™ 1701-E
CATALOG $19.95
LTD ED SIGNED & # PRINTS OT 2,500
$40.00

SciPubTech

Deep Space Nine Poster
Poster Qt.____ @ $19.95 each _____
Limited Edition Poster
Poster Qt.____ @ $40.00 each _____
U.S.S. Enterprise NCC-1701-E Poster
Poster Qt.____ @ $19.95 each _____
Limited Edition Poster
Poster Qt.____ @ $40.00 each _____
U.S.S. Enterprise NCC-1701 Poster
Poster Qt.____ @ $14.95 each _____
Limited Edition Poster
Poster Qt.____ @ $30.00 each _____
$4 Shipping U.S. Each _____
$10 Shipping Foreign Each _____
Michigan Residents Add 6% Tax _____
TOTAL _____

METHOD OF PAYMENT (U.S. FUNDS ONLY)
❑ Check ❑ Money Order ❑ MasterCard ❑ Visa
Account #

_ _ _ _ - _ _ _ _ - _ _ _ _ - _ _ _ _

Card Expiration Date ____/____(Mo./Yr.)

Your Day Time Phone (____) - _____

_____
Your Signature

SHIP TO ADDRESS:

NAME:_____

ADDRESS:_____

CITY:_____STATE:_____

POSTAL CODE:_____COUNTRY:_____

Mail, Phone, or Fax Orders to:
SciPubTech • 15318 Mack Avenue • Grosse Pointe Park • Michigan 48230
Phone 313.884.6682 Fax 313.885.7426 Web Site http://www.scipubtech.com

ST5196

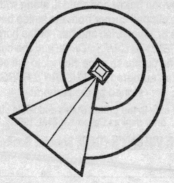

Vulcan, Mount Seleya
Day 6, Seventh Week of Tasmeen,
Year 2247

Dawn hovered over Mount Seleya. A huge *shavokh* glided down on a thermal from the peak, balanced on a wingtip, then soared out toward the desert. Spock heard its hunting call.

Where it stoops, one may find ground water or a soak not too deeply buried, Spock recalled from his survival training. He had no need of such information now. Nevertheless, his gaze followed the creature's effortless flight.

The stairs that swept upward to the narrow bridge still lay in shadow. Faint mist rose about the mountain, perhaps from the snow that capped it, alone of Vulcan's peaks, or perhaps from the lava that bubbled sullenly a thousand meters below. Soon, 40 Eridani A would rise, and the ritual honoring Spock and his agemates would begin.

It was illogical, Spock told himself, for him to assume that all eyes were upon him as he followed his parents.

Instead, he concentrated on his parents' progress. Sustained only by the light touch of Sarek's fingers upon hers, veiled against the coming sunrise, Amanda crossed the narrow span as if she had not conquered her fear of the unrailed bridge only after long meditation.

Few of the many participants from the outworld scientific, diplomatic, and military enclaves on Vulcan could equal her grace. Some had actually arranged to be flown to the amphitheater just to allow them to bypass the bridge that had served as a final defense for the warband that had ruled here in ancient days. Others of the guests crossed unsteadily or too quickly for dignity.

Vertigo might be a reasonable assumption, Spock thought, for beings acclimating themselves to Vulcan's thin air or the altitude of the bridge.

"The air is the air," one of his agemates remarked in the tone of one quoting his elders. "I have heard these *humans* take drugs to help them breathe."

All of the boys eyed the representatives from the Federation as if they were xenobiological specimens in a laboratory. Especially, they surveyed the officials' sons and daughters, who might, one day, be people with whom they would study and work.

"They look sickly," the same boy spoke. His name, Spock recalled, was Stonn. Not only was he a distant kinsman to Sered, he was one of the youths who also eyed Spock as if he expected Spock's human blood to make him fall wheezing to his knees, preferably just when he was supposed to lead his agemates up to the platform where T'Lar and T'Pau would present them with the hereditary—and now symbolic—weapons of their Great Houses. By slipping out early into the desert to undergo his *kahs-wan* ordeal before the others, Spock had made himself forever Eldest among the boys of his year. It was not logical that some, like Stonn, would not forgive him for his presumption, or his survival; but it was so.

A deferential three paces behind his parents and two to the side of Sarek, Spock strode past a series of deeply incised pits—the result of laser cannon fire two millennia back—and up to the entrance of the amphitheater. Two masked guards bearing ceremonial *lirpas* presented arms before his father, then saluted Spock for the first time as an adult. For all his attempts at total control, he felt a little shiver race through him as he returned the salutes as an adult for the first time. The clublike weights that formed the *lirpa* bases shone, a luster of dark metal. The dawn light flashed red on the blades that the guards carried over their shoulders. At the guards' hips, they wore stone-hilted daggers, but no energy weapons—*phasers*—such as a Starfleet officer might wear on duty. Of course, no such weapons might be brought here.

Lady Amanda removed her fingers from her husband's and smiled faintly. "I shall join the other ladies of our House now, my husband, while you bring our son before the Elders. Spock, I shall be watching for you. And I am indeed *very* proud."

As, her gaze told him, *is your father.*

She glided away, a grace note among the taller Vulcans.

Spock fell into step with his father, head high, as if his blood bore no human admixture. *As it was in the beginning...* Silently, he reviewed the beginning of the Chant of Generations as he glided down the stairs.

Everyone in the amphitheater rose. T'Lar, adept and First Student, walked onto the platform. Then, two guards, their *lirpa* set aside for the purpose, entered with a curtained carrying chair. From it, robed in black, but with all the crimsons of the dawn in her brocaded overrobe, stepped T'Pau. She leaned on an intricately carved stick.

Spock's father stepped forward as if to help her.

"Thee is kind, Sarek," said the Elder of their House, "but thee is premature. When I can no longer preside unassisted over this rite, it will be time to release my *katra.*"

Sarek bowed. "I ask pardon for my presumption."

"Courtesy"—T'Pau held up a thin, imperious hand—"is never presumptuous." Her long eyes moved over the people in the amphitheater as if delivering some lesson of her own—but to whom? Carefully, she approached the altar and bowed to T'Lar. "Eldest of All, I beg leave to assist thee."

"You honor me," replied T'Lar.

"I live to serve," said T'Pau, an observation that would have left Spock gasping had he not been getting sufficient oxygen.

Both women bowed, this time to the youths who stood waiting their presentation.

Again, the adept struck the gong.

T'Lar raised both arms, the white and silver of her sleeves falling like great wings. *"As it was in the beginning, so shall it always be. These sons of our House have shown their worthiness . . ."*

"I protest!" came a shout from the amphitheater.

"I protest," Sered declared, "the profanation of these rites. I protest the way they have been stripped of their meaning, contaminated as one might pollute a well in the desert. I protest the way our deepest mysteries have been revealed to *outsiders.*"

T'Pau's eyebrows rose at that last word, which was in the seldom-used invective mode.

"Has thee finished?" asked T'Lar. Adept of *Kolinahr,* she would remain serene if Mount Seleya split along its many fissures and this entire amphitheater crumbled into the pit below.

"No!" Sered cried, his voice sharp as the cry of a *shavokh.* "Above all, I protest the inclusion of an outsider in our rites—yes, as leader of the men to be honored today—when other and worthier men, our exiled cousins, go unhonored and unrecognized."

Sarek drew deep, measured breaths. *He prepares for combat,* Spock realized, and was astonished to feel his own body tensing, alert, aware as he had only been during his *kahs-wan,* when he had faced a full-grown *le-matya* in the deep desert and knew, logically, he could not survive such an encounter. *Fight or flight,* his mother had once called it. That too was a constant across species. *But not here. There must not be combat here.*

"Thee speaks of those who exiled themselves, Sered." Not the slightest trace of emotion tinged T'Pau's voice. "Return lies in their power, not in ours."

"So it does!" Sered shouted. "And so they do!"

He tore off his austere robe. Gasps of astonishment and hisses of outrage sounded as he stood forth in the garb of a Captain of the Hosts from the ancient days. Sunlight picked out the metal of his harness in violent red and exploded into rainbow fire where it touched the gem forming the grip of the ancient energy weapon Sered held—a weapon he had brought, against all law, into Mount Seleya's amphitheater.

"Welcome our lost kindred!" he commanded, and gestured as if leading a charge.

A rainbow shimmer rose about the stage. *Transporter effect,* Spock thought even as it died, leaving behind six tall figures in black and silver. At first glance they were as much like Sered as brothers in their mother's womb. But where Sered wore his rage like a cloak of ceremony, these seemed accustomed to emotion and casual violence.

For an instant no one moved, the Vulcans too stunned by this garish breach of custom, the Federation guests not sure what they were permitted to do. Then, as the intruders raised their weapons, the amphitheater erupted into shouts and motion. From all sides, the guards advanced, holding their *lirpas* at a deadly angle. But *lirpas* were futile against laser rifles.

As the ceremonial guard was cut down, Sarek whispered quick, urgent words to other Vulcans. They nodded. Spock sensed power summoned and joined:

"Now!" whispered the ambassador.

In a phalanx, the Vulcans rushed the dais. They swept across it, bearing T'Pau and T'Lar with them. They, at least, were safe. Only one remained behind. Green blood puddled from his ruined skull, seeping into the dark stone where no blood had flowed for countless generations.

"You dare rise up against me?" Sered shrilled. "One sacrifice is not enough to show the lesser worlds!" He waved his weapon at the boys, at the gorgeously dressed Federation guests. "Take them! We shall make these folk of lesser spirit *crawl.*"

Spock darted forward, not sure what he could do, knowing only that it was not logical to wait meekly for death. And these intruders were not mindless *le-matyas!* They were kindred, of Vulcan stock; surely they could be reasoned with—

As Sered could not. Spock faltered at the sight of the drawn features, the too-bright eyes staring beyond this chaos to a vision only Sered could see. Few Vulcans ever went insane, but here was true madness. Surely his followers, though, clearly Vulcan's long-lost cousins, would not ally themselves with such insanity!

Desperately calm, Spock raised his hand in formal greeting. Surak had been slain trying to bring peace: if Spock fell thus, at least his father would have final proof that he was worthy to be the ambassador's son.

They suddenly seemed to be in a tense little circle of calm. One of the "cousins" pointed at him, while a second nodded, then gestured out into the chaos around them. The language had greatly changed in the sundered years, but Spock understood:

"This one."

"Him."

It may work. They may listen to me. They—

"Get back, son!" a Starfleet officer shouted, racing forward, phaser in outstretched hand, straight at Sered. "Drop that weapon!"

Sered threw back his head. He actually laughed. Then, firing at point-blank range, reflexes swifter than human, he shot the man. The human flared up into flame so fierce that the heat scorched Spock's face and the veils slipped across his eyes, blurring his sight. He blinked, blinked again to clear it, and saw the conflagration that had been a man flash out of existence.

Dead. He's dead. A moment ago alive, and now— Spock stared at Sered across the small space that had held a man, his mind refusing to process what he'd just seen. "Half-blood," muttered Sered. "Weakling shoot of Surak's house. But you will serve—"

"Got him!" came a shout. David Rabin hurled himself into Sered, bringing them both down. The weapon flew from Sered's hand, and Captain Rabin and Sered both scrambled for it. The woman touched it, Sered knocked her hand aside—

And the weapon slid right to Spock. He snatched it up, heart racing faster than a proper Vulcan should permit, and pointed it at Sered.

"Can you kill a brother Vulcan?" Sered hissed, unafraid, from where he lay. "Can you?"

Could he? For an endless moment, Spock froze, seeing Sered's fearless stare, feeling the weapon in his hand. Dimly he was aware of the struggle all around him as the invaders grabbed hostages, but all he could think was that all he need do was one tiny move, only the smallest tightening of a finger—

Can you kill a brother Vulcan?

He'd hesitated too long. What felt like half of Mount Seleya fell on him. Spock thought he heard his father saying, *Exaggeration. Remember your control.*

Then the fierce dawn went black.

Look for STAR TREK Fiction from Pocket Books

Star Trek®: The Original Series

Star Trek: The Motion Picture • Gene Roddenberry
Star Trek II: The Wrath of Khan • Vonda N. McIntyre
Star Trek III: The Search for Spock • Vonda N. McIntyre
Star Trek IV: The Voyage Home • Vonda N. McIntyre
Star Trek V: The Final Frontier • J. M. Dillard
Star Trek VI: The Undiscovered Country • J. M. Dillard
Star Trek VII: Generations • J. M. Dillard
Enterprise: The First Adventure • Vonda N. McIntyre
Final Frontier • Diane Carey
Strangers from the Sky • Margaret Wander Bonanno
Spock's World • Diane Duane
The Lost Years • J. M. Dillard
Probe • Margaret Wander Bonanno
Prime Directive • Judith and Garfield Reeves-Stevens
Best Destiny • Diane Carey
Shadows on the Sun • Michael Jan Friedman
Sarek • A. C. Crispin
Federation • Judith and Garfield Reeves-Stevens
The Ashes of Eden • William Shatner & Judith and Garfield
    Reeves-Stevens
The Return • William Shatner & Judith and Garfield Reeves-
    Stevens

#1 *Star Trek: The Motion Picture* • Gene Roddenberry
#2 *The Entropy Effect* • Vonda N. McIntyre
#3 *The Klingon Gambit* • Robert E. Vardeman
#4 *The Covenant of the Crown* • Howard Weinstein
#5 *The Prometheus Design* • Sondra Marshak & Myrna
    Culbreath
#6 *The Abode of Life* • Lee Correy
#7 *Star Trek II: The Wrath of Khan* • Vonda N. McIntyre
#8 *Black Fire* • Sonni Cooper
#9 *Triangle* • Sondra Marshak & Myrna Culbreath
#10 *Web of the Romulans* • M. S. Murdock
#11 *Yesterday's Son* • A. C. Crispin
#12 *Mutiny on the Enterprise* • Robert E. Vardeman
#13 *The Wounded Sky* • Diane Duane
#14 *The Trellisane Confrontation* • David Dvorkin

Star Trek: The Next Generation®

Encounter at Farpoint • David Gerrold
Unification • Jeri Taylor
Relics • Michael Jan Friedman
Descent • Diane Carey
All Good Things • Michael Jan Friedman
Star Trek: Klingon • Dean W. Smith & Kristine K. Rusch
Star Trek VII: Generations • J. M. Dillard
Metamorphosis • Jean Lorrah
Vendetta • Peter David
Reunion • Michael Jan Friedman
Imzadi • Peter David
The Devil's Heart • Carmen Carter
Dark Mirror • Diane Duane
Q-Squared • Peter David
Crossover • Michael Jan Friedman
Kahless • Michael Jan Friedman
Star Trek: First Contact • J. M. Dillard

#1 *Ghost Ship* • Diane Carey
#2 *The Peacekeepers* • Gene DeWeese
#3 *The Children of Hamlin* • Carnen Carter
#4 *Survivors* • Jean Lorrah
#5 *Strike Zone* • Peter David
#6 *Power Hungry* • Howard Weinstein
#7 *Masks* • John Vornholt
#8 *The Captains' Honor* • David and Daniel Dvorkin
#9 *A Call to Darkness* • Michael Jan Friedman
#10 *A Rock and a Hard Place* • Peter David
#11 *Gulliver's Fugitives* • Keith Sharee
#12 *Doomsday World* • David, Carter, Friedman & Greenberg
#13 *The Eyes of the Beholders* • A. C. Crispin
#14 *Exiles* • Howard Weinstein
#15 *Fortune's Light* • Michael Jan Friedman
#16 *Contamination* • John Vornholt
#17 *Boogeymen* • Mel Gilden
#18 *Q-in-Law* • Peter David
#19 *Perchance to Dream* • Howard Weinstein
#20 *Spartacus* • T. L. Mancour
#21 *Chains of Command* • W. A. McCay & E. L. Flood

Star Trek: Deep Space Nine®

Star Trek®: Voyager™

Star Trek®: New Frontier